ALPHA ACADEMY

IF AT FIRST YOU DON'T SUCCEED, YOU'RE NOT AN ALPHA

NAME: *Charlie Deery*

AGE: *Fourteen and two months*

HOMETOWN: *Hoboken, New Jersey*

KNOWN FOR: *Being a beta.*

GOAL: *To prove I have what it takes to be an alpha.*

SECRET: *Closet tech genius who made the ultimate sacrifice to attend Alpha Academy—my boyfriend.*

YOUR ALPHA MOTTO: *The strong survive.*

MOVERS
& FAKERS

MOVERS & FAKERS

AN ALPHAS NOVEL BY LISI HARRISON

poppy

LITTLE, BROWN AND COMPANY

New York   Boston

Poppy
Little, Brown and Company
Hachette Book Group
237 Park Avenue, New York, NY 10017

For more of your favorite series, go to www.pickapoppy.com

First Edition: April 2010

Poppy is an imprint of Little, Brown and Company
The Poppy name and logo are trademarks of Hachette Book Group, Inc.

Cover design by Andrea C. Uva and Tracy Shaw
Cover photos by Roger Moenks
Author photo by Gillian Crane

alloy**entertainment**
Produced by Alloy Entertainment
151 West 26th Street, New York, NY 10001

ISBN: 978-0-316-03580-4

10 9 8 7 6 5 4 3 2 1
CWO
Printed in the United States of America

For Amelia. Keep writing. Please. ☺

1

"Ready?" Charlie turned to her copilot in the passenger seat and shot her brows skyward, excitement twinkling in her almond-brown eyes. She still couldn't believe where they were, strapped into a Personal Alpha Plane, each zippered into a gold Alphas flight suit with an inspirational quote embroidered along the left sleeve.

Adventure is worthwhile in itself.
—Amelia Earhart

Allie's vivid green eyes met Charlie's. In the light-flooded airplane hangar, they were the exact color of a lime-flavored Jelly Belly. "Can't we just sit here a little longer?" she pleaded, her voice pinched and wavering. Panic-induced perspiration trickled down her porcelain temples like rain on a sidewalk. Charlie examined Allie's profile—

1

ski-slope nose, full rosebud lips, and wide eyes ringed by a perfect fringe of doll-length lashes—and wondered for the millionth time how such a pretty girl had ended up with the confidence of a wet rag.

"No can do, Al. We only have half an hour till class," Charlie reminded her trembling friend. She scooted back against the squishy silver pilot's seat and clicked her safety belt shut, the buckle forming a chunky platinum A.

The golf-cart-size plane looked like a giant Plexiglas soap bubble—it was perfectly round and totally translucent. Charlie was appropriately bubbly herself. She clenched and unclenched her fists, her hands hovering over the touch-screen control panel like she was Beethoven. She scanned her surroundings, making sure they were cleared for take-off.

All around the launchpad, technicians in white jumpsuits and Brazille Enterprises caps were busy making adjustments to the other ninety-nine PAPs.

"Maybe we could do this another time, then?" Allie asked, still trying to weasel her way out of the adventure. She ran a hand through her shiny jet-black hair and cocked her head hopefully at Charlie.

Charlie put a reassuring hand on Allie's jiggling knee. "Don't you want to be the first Alphas to take one of these babies out for a spin?"

At the elite Alpha Academy, where both girls had

managed to survive a month, doing things *first* and doing them the *best* was everything. After all, Shira Brazille's school for exceptional writers, dancers, artists, and inventors was full of girls who had been best and first their whole lives.

"Of course, but this thing is teeny! My Chanel makeup palette is bigger than this." Allie squirted some Purell into her hands and nervously rubbed them together. She stared out the window at the shiny rows of planes lined up in air formation like marbles in a game of Chinese checkers. "Did Shira really say we could be here?"

"Uh-huh." Charlie gloat-grinned, wiggling her fingers to remind Allie. Her nail polish had turned a shade of revved-up red, perfectly matching her mood. "It's my little reward."

The billionaire mogul had called Charlie into her office last night and grudgingly told her that she'd earned a ride in a PAP for having received the first patent at Alpha Academy. Charlie was on the inventor track at school, and she had just trademarked a prototype for saliva-activated nail polish that changed colors based on the pH levels in a person's mouth. Shira predicted the Lick Slicks line of polish would be a major seller for her cosmetics company, X-Chromosome. Charlie had been overjoyed until Shira congratulated her for "dumb luck" by applying existing technology in a "somewhat clever" way.

Charlie and Shira had a more tangled history than Mark Zuckerberg and Facebook's other cofounders: As the daughter of Shira's former assistant, Bee, Charlie had known the international sensation since she was in diapers. A talk-show host whose ratings rivaled Oprah's, Shira was the CEO of not just Brazille Enterprises but various subsidiary companies. She was a household name from Irvine to Indonesia. Over the course of Charlie's life, Shira had become one of the richest, most powerful women in the world. And since day one, she'd also persisted in overlooking Charlie's accomplishments.

"And she said I could bring anyone I wanted. If I'd known you were going to wuss out, I would have picked someone else," Charlie said teasingly.

Lately, Alpha Academy had felt more like a maximum security prison than a school for phenomenally talented girls. Charlie longed to take off and get some breathing room for a few minutes to escape the pressure-cooker vibe. And she knew that once Allie was in the air, she'd feel better, too.

"Okay, okay, fine. I'm not wussing out," Allie sighed. "Let's fly."

"Don't worry. I know what I'm doing." Charlie pulled out her aPod (the glittery rectangle that kept the students of Alpha Academy connected to one another—but not to the rest of the world—and served as a personal remote control for all of the island's technology). The round portals on either side of the plane squeezed shut with a sucking sound, and a map of the @-shaped island appeared on the control screen in front of her, with a blue dot blinking in the launchpad area.

"That's us," Charlie said, pointing at the dot and grinning. She refastened the bobby pin that held back her shaggy brown bangs and prepared for liftoff.

"Now initiating takeoff," said Bee's smooth British-accented voice.

Thanks, Mom, Charlie answered in her head. Usually, hearing Bee's voice was like getting hit on the head with a Nerf bat—momentarily bewildering and kind of unpleasant but not seriously dangerous—but today missing her mother didn't even enter her mind. Today was all about having fun with her new friend.

"If we go down in flames, I want you to know I heart you," Allie said, smiling tightly and gripping the gel-filled arms of her seat hard enough to turn her knuckles white.

"You'll heart me even more when we're airborne." Charlie giggled.

"Now entering air space," Bee informed them as the plane floated smoothly and silently off the ground. Because the carbon-neutral plane ran on a combination of electricity and corn syrup, the cabin was eerily silent; without any jet engine noise, the only sound was the gentle whir of the climate-control system blowing lavender-scented AC across their foreheads.

"Uhmuhgud." Allie loosened her death grip on the armrests and wound her pale arms around one of Charlie's olive ones, squeezing Charlie like two slender boa constrictors.

"Not bad, right?" Charlie grinned, resting her mocha-brown eyes on Allie before moving them back to the control panel.

"Wow." Allie smiled, relaxing back into her chair as the bubble floated upward. "This is almost . . . peaceful." Her green eyes immediately unsquinted, and her lips uncurled from their terrified grimace to their usual puffy O.

"Antigravity technology." Charlie nodded. "Makes for a smooth ride. Pioneered by NASA for space-testing astronauts. Perfected by Brazille Enterprises for Alpha Academy." In this case, Brazille Enterprises meant Charlie Deery, but Charlie didn't want Allie to think she was bragging. And if Shira ever found out how much of the design was actually Charlie's, she would be sent packing faster than a bachelorette after a rose ceremony.

"Here we go!" Charlie whispered with delight as the top of the hangar cracked open like an enormous plastic Easter egg to let them through. Blinding desert sunlight streamed in through the plane's curved windshield, and Charlie took out two pairs of aviator shades from a compartment in the armrest, handing one to Allie and putting the other pair on herself. Shira really had thought of everything.

Just as they were clearing the hangar's octagonal edge, a white camera attached to the ceiling blinked on and angled its lens toward the plane, focusing on them like a personal wink from Shira. *Gotcha!*

"Ugh, there's no escape!" groaned Allie.

"I know," Charlie sighed. "Ah-noying." Ever since Charlie temporarily dismantled the security system to help her bunk-mates meet up with the BBBs (the Billionaire Bra-zille Boys, Shira's five sons and the island's most forbidden fruit), Shira had added hundreds of new cameras and amped up security. The slightest infraction would send an Alpha home, and Shira was watching *everything*.

"At least she hasn't figured out how to float cameras in the sky," Charlie said, finding the silver lining in their float-ing cloud.

She gasped as the plane rose higher; the @-shaped island at the center of a deep blue *faux*cean constructed where the Mojave Desert kissed Nevada still had the power to impress her, even though she'd helped build the thing.

"Bananas," Allie said. "I can't believe we live here."

"Serious-leh," Charlie said, sounding more and more like her new best friend.

Sliding a finger over the map, Charlie steered the plane higher and headed east. Below them, beneath açaí palms,

Joshua trees, and the scrim of wild jungle overgrowth, were the twenty houses where one hundred Alphas slept, studied, schemed, and suffered. Each glass-domed rooftop glittered like a snow globe and sported the signature of a different inspirational woman. They passed Virginia Woolf, Michelle Obama, Oprah, Martha Stewart, J. K. Rowling, Mother Teresa, and finally their own house, Jackie O. Farther out, past Shira's house and the rest of the buildings, gleaming white beaches sparkled against clear blue water.

"Let's cruise lower and see what's happening at the Pavilion." Allie's fear of flying had vanished. Instead she stared openmouthed through the translucent floor of the plane, scanning the ground for Alphas and Brazilles.

"Roger that." It was good to see Allie being enthusiastic about something. Lately, the easygoing songstress had been acting strangely jumpy, like a mouse caught in a trap.

Charlie adjusted the plane's controls and circled to the right, flying past the vertical farm and the Buddha-shaped Zen Center, beyond the harp-shaped Music Hall and the Dionysus dance space dangling high above the junglelike dice hanging from an invisible rearview mirror. Soon the Pavilion rose up in front of them, a skinny oblong structure with white winglike awnings extending from either side, flapping to provide breezy slices of shade. It was lunchtime, and dozens of Alpha girls dressed in matching metallics were lounging around on the shaded lawn.

"Go closer—let's make sure they see us!" Allie studied the ground below to try to spot the blow-outs and ponies that belonged to their friends. "Does this thing have a horn?"

"Lemme see . . ." Charlie pushed a tiny picture of a bird on the touch-screen controls and the plane made a cute chirping noise. "Guess so!" Charlie waved to the Alphas on the lawn forty feet below them.

"Ariella looks so jealous," crowed Allie, pointing at the statuesque platinum blonde squinting up at them in awe. Ariella von Slivovitz was a Russian heiress who had revolutionized the art of cake decorating. She did more with spun sugar than Picasso did with paint. Ariella waved back and beckoned to Ingrid Santana to check out the plane. A Frida Kahlo look-alike minus the bushy eyebrows, Ingrid was a budding marine biologist whose remixes of orca whale songs had won a Grammy last year. "And check out Maxine Montrose—our picture's gonna go viral." Maxine, a voluptuous redheaded photographer, had already attached a telephoto lens to her aPod and was busily snapping pictures of Charlie and Allie floating above them.

Swooping closer to the building, Charlie spotted a figure sitting on a narrow rooftop balcony. She squinted behind her aviators to try to get a better look. The heat-rippled sky revealed the figure to be male—which meant Brazille.

And he was holding a guitar.

Darwin.

Perfect, thought Charlie, unable to pull her gaze away from the hazel-eyed, floppy-haired boy in front of her. Darwin was the last person she wanted to see right now. Shira's musically inclined fourteen-year-old son was Charlie's ex, and their past was more checkered than gingham.

Allie squeaked, and Charlie knew she had spotted him, too. Charlie and Allie shared more than a bedroom— they both had a weakness for Darwin's sun-kissed skin, the adorable freckle above his lip, and his habit of chewing cinnamon-scented toothpicks.

But Charlie had given all that up. Shira wanted her Alphas to focus on school and her sons to date *appropriate* girls. So Charlie had struck the only deal she could: In order to attend Alpha Academy (and stay in physical proximity to Darwin), she had to break up with him, ending a lifelong friendship and sacrificing the only love she'd ever known. Not only that, but she had to give up her mom, too. As a condition of Charlie's enrollment, Shira had forced Bee to resign.

"I'm going to get closer," Charlie said, her voice cracking. She looked over at Allie to see if she'd noticed, but Allie was oblivious, staring moonily at Darwin through twenty, then ten, then five feet of air like her eyes were missiles and he was the target.

Darwin looked up from his guitar, pushing his naturally highlighted waves out of his face and staring through Charlie like she was cellophane. His puppy-dog eyes zeroed in on Allie and fastened onto her like Velcro.

Ouch. Charlie blinked hard. When would her tear ducts get the memo that she and Darwin were yesterday's news?

The extended memo was that lately, Darwin and Allie had been hanging out. As recently as a couple of weeks ago, it had made Charlie crazy. But slowly, she'd gotten used to it. Sort of. And Allie had become a good friend, which was the most important thing.

"Hi Darwin," Allie sighed. She pressed a pale slender hand against the windshield, and Darwin put his hand up to mirror hers. Allie looked forlorn, as if she were separated from Darwin by an ocean and not just a piece of Plexiglas. Ever since the night Allie and Darwin met up in the underground tunnels and Shira had nearly busted everyone, she'd been laying low, unable to see him.

Charlie felt a tickling stab of jealousy in the pit of her stomach, but the knife was duller than it used to be. Mostly, she just felt sad.

Darwin's lips drooped like a wilting flower arrangement as the plane shifted a few inches away in a gust of wind.

"You miss him, huh?" she asked Allie, pulling the plane back up just as a rooftop camera blinked in their direction. Charlie's boiling jealousy of Allie had cooled and was quickly being replaced by concern. Ever since Shira had gone camera crazy and made the island into her own personal version of *Big Brother*, Allie had seemed so low—almost lost. Charlie glanced at Darwin one last time before arcing the plane away, but his eyes were already as lifeless as the buttons on a Raggedy Andy doll.

"Uh-huh." Allie sighed, shrugging her shoulders in defeat.

"It's tough being at a new school with new people and then—"

"The cameras!" wailed Allie, covering her face with her hands. "I feel like I'm being watched every single second!"

"You are," said Charlie, tucking a long mahogany strand of hair behind her ear.

"And Darwin keeps texting, but what can I do?"

"Nothing. You're right to be careful. Shira's dying to kick more of us out." A brooding silence wrapped around them like a sleeping bag as Charlie thought about it more. Her nomadic childhood as part of Shira's entourage had given her a lot: world travel, brilliant private tutors who nurtured her love of math and science, access to all of Shira's amazing resources and technology, and of course the chance to bond with Darwin. But being a part of Shira's entourage had deprived her of a lot, too: Charlie had never lived anywhere long enough to have a place that felt like home, and she'd never had a chance to form anything but the most shallow connections with other girls.

Cruising the plane over the lightbulb-shaped lab where she did her experiments, Charlie felt her heart rev a little faster. The recycled glass building shot up from the jungle like a giant albino mushroom. It was where she felt like she belonged. She squinted through the semi-opaque white walls and smiled when she saw Dr. G, her lab mentor, bent over some slides of her latest project, a spray-foam that dried stronger than cement. With any luck, the foam would be used to build houses for the world's poor. If she had the lab as a home and Allie as a best friend, Charlie would survive here—maybe even flourish. Even without Darwin.

She stole another glance at Allie, who looked lower than the ocean floor. Charlie tried to imagine how she would feel if the situation were reversed. What if Darwin had broken up with *her*? She hoped he would want her to be happy, to move on.

It was crazy, but Charlie realized she *wanted* Allie and Darwin to be together now. Life at the Academy was more competitive than Olympic figure skating, more stressful than the PSATs. Succeeding here could turn you from ordinary to infamous, from mousy to magnetic, from Lisa Simpson to Jessica Simpson. And surviving here was way more likely with a friend on your side.

If Charlie couldn't be with Darwin herself, then at least she could find a way to make her best friend and her boyfriend—or, rather, boy "friend"—happy.

"Let's take her in," she said. Charlie pushed the Twizzler-shaped icon on the PAP's touchscreen and Bee's voice acknowledged her selection as the plane angled through the crystalline sky. "Now preparing for landing. We hope you enjoyed your flight on Alpha Airways."

"Roger that," said Allie, pasting on a brave smile.

Soon, if Charlie had anything to say about it, Allie would have something real to smile about.

2

THEATER OF DIONYSUS
HONE IT: FOR DANCERS
MONDAY, SEPTEMBER 20TH
2:18 P.M.

As the elevator soared above the tree line toward the floating glass cube of the dance studio, Skye squinted her Tiffany box–blue eyes, searching Alpha Island for any signs of a potential audience. Here and there, yellow-bellied finches and orange-and-purple parakeets flitted among the palm fronds. On the westernmost edge of the island, where the curved tail of the island's @-shape formed a marshy isthmus, she spotted two muses gathering shells along the water's edge. Actual Alphas were apparently in scarce supply during class periods—hypercompetitive, 99th percentile, leaders-of-tomorrow types didn't ditch class without a good reason. The glass floor of the studio meant that anyone with the luck to be out of doors and in view of the studio could watch a performance, but so far, it looked like Skye's comeback would be witnessed by the bun-heads alone.

Correction: the bun-heads and at least three of Shira's cameras.

The elevator opened with a chime, followed by the British voice recording: "Welcome to the Dionysus practice hall, where dance is your pleasure." An excited shiver rippled through Skye's lithe torso. She stepped out of the elevator onto the clear rubberized glass floor of the studio and took a deep whiff of the organic eucalyptus/lemon thyme spray-solvent manufactured by Brazille Enterprises. Most dance studios smelled of corroded toe shoes and sweaty leotards, but this one smelled like inspiration. A tiny, tasteful disco ball hung from the ceiling, bouncing mini-rainbows off the floor and onto the walls.

Triple, Prue, and Ophelia waved at her from the barre, where they were yawning through their usual *battement tendu*, each girl clad in a slightly different shade of metallic leo topped by a floaty chiffon dance skirt. Skye chin-thrust a greeting in return, quickly shedding her sweatsuit and revealing her silver dance cami and shirred silver boy shorts. Showing off her glutes made her feel powerful and confident, something her elephant-size ankle bandage did not. She suppressed a smile as all six eyebrows at the barre shot up in appraisal of her missing ankle brace and butt-hugging outfit.

Prepare to be jealous, girls.

With Skye's regulation Alpha-issued dance attire, there

was nothing out of place. Her bun was the tightest and slickest in the room, preventing her white-blond curls from whipping around and inspiring her to attempt crazy feats of experimental self-expression during class. Her dance sleeves, the trademark accessory of the old Skye, were now charred around the edges, tucked away in a shoebox under her bed. She'd tried to burn them on the beach one night as part of her commitment to impressing Mimi, their instructor, who had a drill sergeant's soul wrapped in the body of a world-class choreographer. Unfortunately, the sparkly lycra/viscose blend refused to burst into flame, so she'd watched the sleeves smoke and smolder for a while before stamping them out and giving up. Her body was toned and trim from weeks of salmon, egg whites, greens, and five hundred sit-ups a day, and thanks to countless hours of strengthening exercises, her ankle was good as new—better, even.

She looked around at her fellow dancers lunging in deep quad stretches against the barre, picturing herself dancing among them, her moves just as tight as her severe bun. Today, she was sure she would finally impress Mimi, who would applaud her for sticking to the routine, for memorizing it perfectly while sitting on the sidelines. In just a few minutes, she'd finally get the praise she so desperately needed to regain her confidence.

"Lookin' serious, Sleeveless!" joked Prue, winding an

errant strand of red hair around her messy bun. "You're like Britney on her comeback tour."

Skye glared at the Nicole Kidman wannabe. The comparison to Britney hit her like a punch in the stomach; she'd sprained her ankle, not shaved her head and lost her mind! She made a mental note never to ask Prue to dance backup for her once she'd made it big. *You have no idea how seriously I'm about to dominate this studio.*

"We'll see," smirked Triple. She rolled her eyes like she knew something Skye didn't . . . like Skye had been the butt of every joke among the bun-heads during her ankle-healing absence.

Triple, short for Triple Threat, was Skye's bunk-mate in the Jackie O house along with Charlie and Allie J. Skye wished she could undo whatever computer error was responsible for housing two dancers in the same dorm; putting up with the Goody Tap-shoes "mo-dan-tress" day and night was like wearing a pair of too-tight toe shoes: uncomfortable at best, scream-inducing at worst.

"That all you got?" muttered Skye, turning her back on Triple and surveying the room. She wasn't in the mood for the girl's mega-negative vibes.

She had been running through the steps of Mimi's latest in her head all morning, along with some of Shira's inspirational Alpha phrases like "there's nothing prettier than hard work paying off," and "when in doubt, be the best." For the last two weeks, ever since Shira had quadrupled the number of surveillance cameras on the island, it had been all dance and no fun for Skye. But today it was finally going to pay off. Skye had been doing everything possible to honor her HADs (Hopes and Dreams), which she'd written on slips of paper and stuffed inside the lavender ballet slipper her mother, the once-famous prima ballerina Natasha Flailenkoff, had given her the day she had received her acceptance package from school.

HAD No. 1:   *To stay at Alpha Academy.*
HAD No. 2:   *To stay on Charlie's good side (no more blabbing Jackie O secrets to bun-heads!).*
HAD No. 3:   *To heal and dance by morning.*
HAD No. 4:   *To swear off boys until graduation.*
HAD No. 5:   *To be the best.*

The slipper had worked for Natasha, and so far Skye had managed to keep all her HADs alive. For the past week, the elimination assembly the Jackie O's all feared had not materialized. Shira had been called away on urgent business, and school had chugged along as usual in her absence. Paranoia was running high, what with the additional eyes glued to every ceiling, but Skye had kept her head in the game. She had earned Charlie's forgiveness for bringing dancers into the tunnel by promising to come clean to Shira and take the blame if it ever came up.

The hardest HAD to honor was actually a spectacular success. For the past week, she had ignored Taz's endlessly flattering, dangerously tempting stream of text messages. Shira's most kissable son, famous for dating models and starlets, was cryogenically frozen in Skye's heart; she would only thaw him out once she had proven herself to Mimi. The only thing Skye needed to do now was earn the title of best dancer at the Academy. Triple had Mimi wrapped around her calloused toes, but today all that was about to change. The new, disciplined Skye was about to demote Triple Threat to Double Trouble.

Two earsplitting hand-claps and the jangling of twenty thin gold bracelets announced Mimi's entrance. Intimidating and gorgeous in a low-cut black leotard and an electric blue dovetail skirt that showed off her burnished caramel skin, Mimi inspired awe and fear in equal measure. Skye plastered a toothy smile on her face and stood at attention next to the barre, trying to look nonchalant even though her future at Alpha Academy depended on today's performance.

A few more dancers had arrived moments before, still in chat mode as they unzipped their hoodies. Mimi narrowed her golden eyes at them, her mouth pursed in a glossed, furious O.

"Mouths closed, toes pointed! If I wanted to hear what you had to say, I would have become a shrink and not a choreographer!" Mimi made eye contact with Skye and acknowledged her with a slight tilt of her chignoned head. "Show me how you feel with your bodies! Music . . . on! Up-tempo, major key, updated funk!"

A half second later, the studio's voice-activated music library made its selection, and the room was a swirl of drums, horns, and booty-shaking soul. "Positions, please!" Mimi yelled. "Sleeves, far right, front corner! Let's see what you can bring to the sequence. We're picking back up from the step-ball-change, dancers! Ah-one, ah-two, ah-one two three four!"

The floor of the studio bounced with the pressure of the sequence, a series of jetés and leaps combined with the hip-pops and boom-shaka-laka drop-and-recovers in a kind of hip-hop-meets-classical-dance hybrid. Skye felt the rhythm of the dance reverberate through her legs and spread through her whole body. She knew every twirl, every flip of the hand and roll of the hips, because she'd studied them so carefully while sitting on the sidelines. Her muscles twanged like the strings of a guitar. She could make them sing any song she wanted today. And she wasn't even tempted to throw in a Skye-style flourish. Out of the corner of her eye, she saw Prue and Triple hip-thrust-and-turn and up-two-three-four in perfect synchronicity with her. Her body and spirit soared with the music as she matched her fellow danc-ers step for step. Mimi's appraising eyes rested on her, but she continued to look straight ahead, smiling.

She was back.

When the music stopped, Skye let her shoulders roll back and planted her feet in second position, panting from exertion. She'd nailed it.

"Sleeves, again. Solo this time," said Mimi. "Music, repeat!"

On top already! Skye danced the sequence again, careful not to incorporate any of her usual head bobs, extra hip swivels, or anything else where her desire to express herself overshadowed the routine. Finally, she was doing the thing that set her free, that made her feel beautiful, like she was on this earth for a reason beyond boys, beyond besties. It was the way she always felt at Body Alive, her old dance studio, where she was such a huge star that her instructor, Madame P, left her in charge of the entire class during pee breaks. The drums throbbed through her, guiding her switch-twirl, her body as stretchy and pliable as a rubber band and as strong as a racehorse, powering through every move.

When the music stopped and Skye dropped her arms, a smattering of grudging applause erupted from the dancers. *That showed them.*

Skye smiled, trying to look modest while soaking up admiration she knew she had earned. She raised an eyebrow at Triple, feeling cocky and letting it show. Triple looked away, and Skye could almost smell defeat oozing from her invisible, exfoliated pores. *Ha!*

"Nice kick at the end, Skye," said Prue, flashing her a thumbs-up.

Skye thought she heard her aPod flash from the corner of the studio, where she'd left it stuffed under her hoodie. Couldn't Taz leave her alone for half an hour? She quickly replanted her gaze on Mimi.

"Sleeves, can you tell us what you were thinking about while you were dancing?"

That I was onstage at Madison Square Garden with a hundred thousand people chanting my name? That I was kicking Triple's conceited butt? That I was the best? None of these answers would do, obviously.

"I was thinking about how much I still had to learn from everyone, from you, and how I wanted to stick to the essence of the routine. And I thought about the *tradition* of jazz dancing, the *fundamentals*, and how important it is to master those core moves before I make my own additions." It was butt-kissy, but it was the kind of answer Mimi would eat up. Skye smiled brightly at her instructor, anticipating long-awaited words of praise.

"And that," said Mimi, turning on the three-inch heel of her Capezio Salsa Moderna, facing the dancers gathered on one side of the studio, "is why Sleeves is out of sync with the music."

What?

"The mind should be quiet when dancing. *Feel*, don't

think! Your answer was still all about *you*, Sleeves, about where *you* fit in. It needs to be about the *dance*, about your spirit, not your ego. Andrea is the only one of you who dances with her spirit." Mimi looked over at Triple Threat, who was suddenly all smiles and noticeably puffed up like a person with a shellfish allergy who'd just downed a sushi boat.

Andrea? Triple Threat?! But she's a dance-bot! She has no passion! Skye blinked back tears and swallowed a mouthful of rage.

"Andrea, please dance the sequence solo. Music, re—peat!"

As the bass pumped out of the speakers and Triple moved in her usual robotic, uninspired style, Skye's eyes wandered toward her sweatshirt crumpled in the corner of the room and then returned to the somber group of her fellow dancers, all of whom nodded as if they actually saw a difference between the two dancers, as if Triple really *was* better. *Traitors! Philistines!*

That was when a realization hit Skye, more powerfully and offensively than the reek of two weeks of unwashed leotards: No matter what she did, no matter how hard she worked or how much she tried to suppress her own style, she would never convince Mimi that she had passion. Triple would always be number one, because Mimi had already made up her mind.

Then what's the point in trying? Skye watched Triple

dance, but instead of music, she heard the beating of her own heart thundering in her ears. Mimi hated her, and dancing at Alpha Academy was nothing more than adapting to new forms of humiliation. Skye would never achieve her HADs from within these transparent walls. She wasn't going to make her mother proud and become a world-famous dancer.

And just like that, as if a jangly hand-clap from Mimi had stopped her in the middle of a routine, Skye reset her priorities.

You win, Triple. You can have all of this.

"Class dismissed!" barked Mimi. "Work on it, Sleeves!"

Skye looked at the floor and nodded, vowing that nobody in this room would get the satisfaction of seeing her cry. By the time she had crossed the room to retrieve her pile of warm-up clothes and check her phone for forbidden texts, it was obvious what the next step was. If Plan A fails, move on to Plan B.

Plan Boys.

3

JACKIE O
ALLIE A'S BED
MONDAY, SEPTEMBER 20TH
8:46 P.M.

The sleeping quarters of the Jackie O House reverberated with the soothing sounds of Peruvian wind instruments, but Allie A. Abbott was anything but soothed. Next to a nightstand littered with gum wrappers, Allie lay curled up like a comma on her bed. Her Alpha-issued gold nightgown was more than warm enough for the September night, but Allie shivered as her mind ran through the events of the past two weeks. She rolled over, trying not to think about it.

Allie looked around at her fellow Jackie O's, each girl sprawled on her canopied bed in a posture of pseudo-relaxation. After nearly three weeks on Alpha Island, Allie felt certain that nobody ever *really* let their guard down at Alpha Academy. The girls chosen to attend Shira's new school had grown up working their butts off to be the biggest fish in their small ponds, and now that they were gathered together, the place was a shark tank.

Skye lay in the bed to Allie's right, her blond wavelets reaching almost to her butt, cracking her wrists in bed and brooding about dance class. Allie could hear her muttering, *"One-two-three-four, I'm not dancing anymore"* under her breath as she flexed and pointed her feet. Skye's champagne-shiny cami and boy shorts skimmed a perfect dancer's body, lean and toned like a cheetah, capable of executing any combination of moves. Allie knew she was mega-talented—Skye was just going through a post-injury setback. To Allie's left sat Charlie, cross-legged and serious, hunched over a laptop and absorbed in a furious bout of pre-sleep coding for one of her ingenious technological projects. She chewed her lower lip in concentration, and Allie marveled at how well she pulled off her geek-chic style: Charlie's mahogany-brown hair, piled high on her head in a messy bun, perfectly complemented her nerd-core rectangular black plastic glasses. Luckily, she only needed them for close-up stuff like coding and reading.

Whether it was an innate talent from birth or from growing up around Shira, dreaming big was something Charlie knew how to do. It had been Charlie who had arranged for Allie to meet up with Darwin in the island's secret underground tunnel for the best few minutes of Allie's life so far: kissing Darwin's pillowy, cinammon-scented lips. It would be Charlie—the girl who had made life at Alphas not just livable but truly fun—who she would hurt most of all if the secret of her middle initial was revealed.

Allie A, aspiring mall model, had faked her way into Alpha Academy by pretending to be Allie J, the famous eco-songwriter pop star.

And as of two weeks ago, Shira knew all about it.

In a fit of paranoia, Allie reached up and patted the kohl-mole above her upper lip, a crucial part of her disguise that she had to stealthily redraw with eyeliner every morning. Patting her mole was one of the many nut-job tics she'd adopted since she started masquerading as Allie J, whose acceptance letter had been mistakenly sent to Allie's house in suburban Santa Ana, California. Allie J was Allie A's only ticket into the Academy. No way would Shira Brazille ever invite a bubbly blonde whose greatest skill was an encyclopedic knowledge of celebrity culture.

Allie sighed and looked past Charlie to the next bed, home to the sleep-obsessed Andrea. Andrea, aka Triple Threat, came with enough diva-tude for three, but at the moment her energies were devoted to highlighting passages of *From Outback to Riches: The Shira Brazille Story*. *What a kiss-up*, Allie thought, rolling her contact-lens-enhanced eyes.

Finally, Allie's eyes landed on the last bed in the room, where the soap actress Renee had slept before getting kicked out of the Academy for flirting with the Brazille brothers. Renee's empty bed was a daily reminder for Allie that her neck could be next on the chopping block.

Thalia, the Jackie O house muse, stood in the back of

the bedroom and pushed a button on the touch-screen projector embedded in the wall. The windows that moments ago revealed a clear, dark ocean; the tops of açaí palm trees; and all twelve constellations of stars were suddenly filled with Thalia's carefully curated photographs of inspirational women. Allie leaned against a stack of pillows and watched Princess Diana working with land-mine victims, Oprah hugging African children, Queen Noor of Jordan giving a speech at the UN, Diane von Furstenberg sketching a design on a huge piece of butcher paper. Each picture came with a tagline trademarked by Brazille Industries for use in Shira's wildly popular Female Empowerment Workshops (FEWs).

Allie watched the slideshow absently, hoping nobody else could hear the frantic sounds her jaw made as she chomped on piece after piece of cinnamon gum.

Absolute focus! (Chomp chomp chomp)
Leaders of tomorrow! (Smack)
Positivity leads to excellence! (Crinkle—new piece)
Hit your mark! (Slobber, drool)
Aspire to greatness! (Pop—oops!)

The slideshow was nice in theory, but the only words running through Allie's brain were *fraud*, *fake*, *liar*, and *busted*.

Allie looked up at the glass-domed ceiling and felt like a creature on display in a human-size terrarium. Not for the first time, she pictured everyone she knew back home—namely her ex-boyfriend, Fletcher, and her ex-bestie Trina, but her parents, too, even her old teachers—watching her squirm in a hidden-camera mocumentary called *The Joke's on Allie*.

Now that Shira knew the truth about who Allie was (and who she wasn't), her paranoia level was permanently at code orange. Because the only thing more tiring than lying to everyone was trying to figure out why Shira had kept her secret for so long. It had been a week since Allie had come face-to-face with the real Allie J in Shira's office, so what was she still doing here? And even if she *were* staying, what kind of greatness could she possibly aspire to? Being the best liar in school? Root maintenance that rivaled Madonna's? Faking her way through life?

As the New Age elevator music careened toward a crescendo, Allie's exhausted mind groped for reasons she wouldn't be kicked out. Maybe Allie J snubbed Shira by not wanting to attend the Academy, and Shira needed Allie to stay in order to save face? That was the only logical explanation for why Shira didn't kick her out last week, for why the barefoot songstress had not made a follow-up appearance, and why life on the island was Alphas as usual. Or maybe the encounter with Allie J hadn't really happened? Could it have been a dream, just a vivid hallucination during her fainting spell in Shira's office? Allie's nerves were so frayed that anything was possible.

"Hey, Chew-baca!" Skye whisper-yelled. "Puh-leeze quit chewing. I bit it hard today, and sleep is all I have to look forward to."

"Sorry," Allie mumbled, spitting out her latest piece of gum and wrapping it up. The slideshow had ended without her even noticing.

"You can always look forward to the challenge of keeping up with me tomorrow," Triple sneer-snorted at Skye from underneath her blackout eye mask. The words *rock star* were embroidered on the outside in screaming pink letters, apparently affirming her unshakable ego even while she slept. Triple pointed an OPI Russian Debutante Red foot, and Allie grimaced at Triple's calloused feet hanging off the edge of her bed. Didn't the girl know that pathogens could affix themselves to so much dead skin?

"Thanks, Triple," snapped Skye. "But I'd rather focus on trying to drum up some excitement around here."

"My excitement is with my craft." Triple raised a corner of her eye mask to glare in Skye's direction, flipped her flawless blow-out so it fanned out over her pillow, and settled back into bed as if to say, *The Diva Has Spoken*.

As Skye and Charlie shared a simultaneous eye roll, Allie wished for the millionth time that she could just tell them her secret and move on, knowing they were friends with her *for her*. She had almost confessed a thousand times this week, but every time she came close to telling the truth, there was always a better reason not to. She even had a running tally in her head:

ALMOST FESSED UP	GAVE UP
Immediately after meeting Allie J in Shira's office. Everyone would find out soon, anyway—she may as well be the first to break the news.	Everyone was in deep REM sleep by the time she returned to the Jackie O House. Why wake them?
The next morning during breakfast, when she was sure the ax was about to fall.	It would be impolite to ruin everyone's day before they'd digested their breakfasts.
While getting ready for bed with Charlie in the Jackie O bathroom.	They were in the middle of a serious cuticle convo about the hottest nail-polish colors this season—Kelly green and lemon yellow. It would have been rude to change the subject!
While doing ankle-strengthening moves with Skye. (Allie didn't need them, but she wanted to give Skye some moral support.)	They had been talking about friendship, and Skye remarked that the worst thing a friend could do was lie to another friend. It kind of killed the mood.
The next night, during one of the Jackie O's whispered drool-fests over the Brazille brothers.	When she thought of Darwin, panic and lust in combination made her nauseated. She took out her Purell and tried to focus on killing germs instead of her reputation.
Every day thereafter.	If Shira wasn't telling, why should Allie?

Allie hadn't seen Darwin alone since her encounter with the real Allie J. Not only did the potential revelation of her real identity make it impossible for her to lock lips with a clear conscience, but Shira had installed cameras *everywhere* to watch the girls' every move. Allie needed to stay out of any situation that smelled like trouble. And Darwin reeked of it.

Shira's number-one rule for Alpha girls was *No Fraternizing with the Brazille Boys.* They were to share classes and ideas—not spit. But avoiding Darwin wasn't easy, and as his texts grew increasingly persistent, Allie's dodges had become increasingly lame.

DARWIN TRIES	ALLIE LIES
Wanna meet in the tunnel tonight?	Can't. Writing a song about composting.
Where R U?	Circulating a petition about our towels. Plush cotton weave is so 2009—hemp towels save trees!
R U avoiding me?	No way! Why would you think that???

Now all Allie had of Darwin was her gum, a pathetic facsimile of his cinnamon-scented toothpicks. No gum was sweet enough to match the flavor of his kiss, the feel of his arms around her waist, the thrill of knowing she would see him soon, and the chance that their relationship would bloom like the tropical flowers on Alpha Island—wild, exotic, yet engineered for perfection.

Ping!

Hoping it was Darwin—and then praying it wasn't—Allie leapt for her aPod. She checked the glowing screen, half hoping, half dreading a sweet good-night kiss via text—or worse, another request to sneak out that she would have to refuse.

But it wasn't Allie's aPod beeping. Sweeping aside a heap of gum wrappers, she laid her aPod on her bedside table and looked around the dark room to see whose face was glowing.

"Taz!" Allie could see the white of Skye's smile lit by her aPod's mini-screen. "I'm emoticon-ing him back this time. Now that dance is dead to me, I have nothing to lose."

"Not that you'll be able to actual-leh *see* him," Allie reminded her.

"These cameras are *such* a drag." Skye groaned. "The past two weeks have been deader than MJ." She moonwalked her fingers across her comforter and looked up at the stars. "RIP, Michael," she added with a sigh.

Allie envied Skye's single-mindedness. Whether it was dancing or Taz, Skye had her eyes on the prize. She wondered if she would ever manage to be that way about anything. Split-end maintenance didn't count as a passion, did it?

"Allie-oop," Skye whispered to Allie, "no text from Darwin?"

"He texted earlier," she said. "I'd love to see him, but I'm too freaked out." *For so many reasons.*

She looked over at Charlie, who was still tapping away on her laptop. Even though Charlie was her best friend at the Academy, Allie wasn't always totally convinced she was over Darwin. After all, they'd been together for years. If she were in Charlie's position, Allie wasn't sure she would be so accommodating.

"You can all thank me later," Charlie announced, her face blue in the glow of her computer screen. "I've just finished writing my six-point plan of attack."

"What are you attacking?" Skye cracked her neck first to the right, then to the left, and shot Allie a *Charlie's lost it* look.

Charlie flashed Allie a mischievous grin. This was going to be good, Allie could feel it. Charlie could do things regular Alphas just couldn't. Flying a PAP wasn't even the half of it.

Charlie straightened up behind her laptop. "I'm going to find a way to help Allie see Darwin. And Skye, you'll be able to see Taz. In fact, *any* Alpha girl can see *any* Brazille boy—if my plan works."

Everyone glanced over at Triple, but she was out cold under her ROCK STAR eye mask.

"Serious-leh? You mean you're going to find a way to get rid of the cameras?" Allie felt her face flush, both at the possibility of seeing Darwin again and at the awesomeness that was Charlie Deery. How could she have doubted Charlie's sincerity about Darwin? Charlie was everything that Trina wasn't—loyal to a fault.

"Uh-huh." Charlie beamed a thousand-watt smile straight at Allie. "Tomorrow."

Skye jumped out of bed and did a spontaneous pirouette. "Ah-mazing! Charlie, you're a lifesaver." She sat back down in her bed, frantically tapping on her aPod. "I'm texting Taz right now."

"What are you writing?" Allie asked. She wished she could be as in-the-moment as Skye, but she suddenly felt as if she'd just swallowed a bag of Pop Rocks with a Diet Coke chaser—full of fizzy, slightly scary expectation.

"I'm asking if he's free tomorrow night. I'm not the kind of girl who takes her time." Skye pointedly raised her eyebrows at Allie.

"You should text Darwin," agreed Charlie in a gentle voice. "I mean, if you want."

Allie nodded, shivering at the possibility. Charlie was the best! If she could just feel the warmth of Darwin's hand in hers and maybe even make contact with his soft lips, she knew she'd be able to survive the anxiety of living a lie.

"I will. But first, lemme see the plan!" Allie rolled out

of her bed and bounced onto Charlie's, almost knocking the laptop to the floor as she squeezed Charlie in a happy hug, the kind she used to give her favorite stuffed animal, Mr. Moose McCuddles, back when she was seven and the phrase *identity theft* didn't even exist.

"Okay, so you know how Shira's always asking me to spy for her? That's step one . . . ," Charlie began.

Staring at Charlie's carefully calibrated spreadsheet, Allie brushed her secret back under the rug of her unconscious, where it couldn't torture her so much. After all, if Shira really wanted Allie out, she would already be gone. Wouldn't she?

4

BRAZILLE RESIDENCE
FRONT PORCH
TUESDAY, SEPTEMBER 21ST
5:37 P.M.

T-Minus 29:00

Like the mogul herself, Shira's front door was larger-than-life. The enormous slab of Brazillian Rosewood gleamed in the late-afternoon light. Charlie laid her hand on the nine-foot door, trying to remember how much Bee had told her it was worth. *Forty thousand? Eighty?* The sums were so large that Charlie couldn't keep them all straight. A pair of white butterflies danced in front of the jasmine that crept along Shira's fence, and Charlie took a deep breath of the fragrant air. *Calm down, Charlie, you can do this.*

Nobody knew Shira better than Charlie did, except Bee, but the stakes were high. If she got caught, she'd be shipped off to boarding school in Hoboken, New Jersey, faster than a PAP could reach 40,000 feet.

The plan, focus on the plan! Charlie checked her watch for the twentieth time.

So far, things had gone off without a hitch. At exactly 5:29, Charlie had sent a text.

Charlie: I've been a good spy. I have a name for you. Need to see you today.

Being Shira's ex-assistant's daughter had its perks. Charlie had Shira's schedule memorized—it helped that her habits had remained relatively unchanged for more than ten years. 5:29 was when Shira's driver dropped her off at home, and at 5:58, she had a nightly conference call with her accountant. What Shira did for the twenty-nine minutes in between was a mystery to Charlie, but whatever it was, it happened at home. Thankfully, Shira's mysterious time slot coincided with Darwin's nightly jog on the beach, so chances were good that Charlie wouldn't have to explain to him what she was doing here.

Charlie pressed Shira's doorbell again and realized she had never entered the house from the front before. For almost her whole life, she'd been a member of Shira's professional family: first, because she came along with Bee, who had keys to the back entrances of all of Shira's properties. Later on, when she was with Darwin, she entered the Brazille house as if she lived there. Now she was on her own, without the backstage pass that came with being part of Shira's entourage. And neither her mother nor Darwin was there to protect her anymore.

T-Minus 26:00

Just when Charlie was starting to hyperventilate from nervousness, the door whooshed open to reveal Fiona, Shira's first assistant (formerly her second assistant, until Bee left).

"Come in, Charlie. Shira will see you now." A thin smile passed quickly over Fiona's lipsticked mouth, as crisply professional as her tailored crepe suit and pumps. They had known each other for years, but it was clear that to Fiona, Charlie was on the outside now.

Charlie stepped inside, feeling faintly ridiculous in her Alpha uniform: a platinum vest, pleated mini in shimmering pewter, champagne-colored blouse with oversize puffed sleeves, and clear knee-high gladiator sandals with massaging soles and no-tan-line technology. All Alpha-issued clothing was light-reflective—Shira wanted her girls to never forget to shine.

Shira's great room was easily large enough to house a jet. One side looked like the swooping wing of an enormous glass seagull, curving and narrowing into a dramatic archway. Charlie hovered near the back wall, which was lined with framed photographs of Shira and the boys. Charlie knew most of the photos by heart—the twins, Taz and Dingo, at six, each missing front teeth, grinning on an Indonesian beach. The one of Melbourne and Darwin fencing in Bath, England, Charlie's mother, Bee, standing off to the side. The one of Sydney, age nine or ten, studying an atlas in the living room of Shira's Park Avenue penthouse.

Charlie peered among the pictures, looking for the one of her with Darwin. Her eyes skimmed past Shira shaking hands with Bill Clinton, Shira with foreign dignitaries at an international conference in Davos, Switzerland, Shira with Oprah and Bono at her End Global Hunger Annual Gala, Shira with Bill and Melinda Gates. . . . Where was the picture from Lake Titicaca? *Aha!*

The second Charlie's eyes landed on the picture of her and Darwin in Bolivia, age six and seven respectively, chewing on stalks of sugarcane with the sparkling lake behind them, she felt the same stab in her stomach she'd felt in the PAP. *Stop torturing yourself, Charlie!* The last thing she needed before lying to Shira was to wonder why she made her deal with the she-devil and traded her boyfriend for a chance to shine.

"Charlie?" Fiona tapped her watch. "Shira's time is valuable."

"Of course," Charlie started, ripping her eyes from the wall. "I'm right behind you."

Mentally replacing the picture of Darwin with one of Allie, Charlie took a deep breath and kept walking, forcing her gladiator sandals along Shira's Oriental rug until Darwin's face slid away from her like a bug on her windshield.

T-Minus 18:00

Fiona led her through a sliding glass door and out to the backyard. The smell of honeysuckle, manure, and the ocean filled Charlie's nostrils. On one side of the yard was Shira's garden, with all manner of exotic flora. There were giant purple roses of Sharon, wild bougainvillea in every color of the rainbow, huge sunflowers whose heads bobbed and dipped in the breeze like they were singing backup at an Amy Winehouse concert. On the other side, flanking the gently rolling grass hills that led down to Shira's docked sailboats at the water's edge, were the stables and a small barn. Which apparently was where they were headed.

Inside the barn, dust motes danced in the refracted golden light of early evening. It smelled loamy and musty and very distinctly of horse pee. Charlie hadn't been to the barn in ages. Was it really possible that this dank, noisy place was Shira's hangout?

"My wittle Cookie mookie! I wuv my wamma, yes I do!" Shockingly, the voice sounded like . . . Shira's. Charlie suppressed a smirk as the mogul came into view in the dim light of the straw-strewn animal pens, filling up the food trough for Cookie, the nasty alpaca who spat at everyone but her.

"And let's give beautiful Bill and plain old Hillary their dinner . . . and—" A gurgling, insistent series of snorts from Althea, a Vietnamese potbellied pig, interrupted Shira's baby-talk monologue as she fed her prized peacocks.

Fiona cleared her throat and stepped out of the shadows of the barn toward Shira, Charlie in tow.

"Hi," Charlie said, noting the mud-smeared rubber boots adorning the feet of one of the richest, most powerful women in the world. Shira had tucked her auburn curls into an Alpha Academy promotional cap, but even in the musty barn she still wore her trademark dark glasses. She pressed her lips together in a thin, tight smile.

"G'day, Charlie."

T-Minus 11:00

Charlie looked up after a quick glance at her aPod timer. Now was when her performance had to be perfect, or she would run out of time and be ushered off the premises before completing the mission.

"I always thought you had someone to do this"—Charlie waved her hand around the whole animal menagerie—"for you."

"Oh, this?" Shira unlatched a pen that housed two lambs covered in sky blue wool. "This, m'dear, is what keeps me sane. Reminds me of the emu farm I was raised on. These little blue lambs were given to me by Ashton and Demi last month—some cloning project they're financing, God knows why."

Stick to your plan, Charlie reminded herself, swallow-nodding. Charlie needed to keep Shira busy with small talk until her 5:58 phone call.

"So, um, my mom sends her regards. She's in school, you know. In England. New South Wales. She's studying art history. She's considering getting her PhD—"

"Is that right?" Shira said absently. She bent down to scoop up a baby quail that had become separated from its brothers and sisters. "And you, Charlie, are you learning anything at this fabulous incubator for talent?"

"I'm learning so much, I can hardly believe it. The teachers here are amazing. This week I'm creating a new circuit system for a teleportation device I'm working on, and you already know about the nail polish—"

"Mmmm." Shira barely responded, focused only on the zebra in the corner stall. "Fiona, make a note to call the vet in the morning. Zorro hasn't touched her food."

"Done." Fiona entered the new task into the clipboard.

"You were saying, Lolly? Full speed ahead, yes? Keeping up with all the gifted girls at the Academy not proving to be too much for you yet, I suppose."

"Actually, no . . ." Charlie trailed off. *This* was the Shira she knew and loathed! When would the woman realize that Charlie had a brain in her head? That she had done more to create the technology on Alpha Island than almost anyone? "I'm managing to hold my own here so far," she said tightly, checking her aPod clock yet again.

T-Minus 5:00 (*Phew!*)

"So, like I was saying, I'm working on this new circuit—

44

the configuration has never been tried successfully before. It requires a crazy amount of CAD coding, so I'm brushing up on that in my spare time. . . ."

Charlie smiled to herself as Shira's face went slack from boredom. Technology was never Shira's strong suit. She paid the bills to create and maintain Alpha Academy's technology wonderland, but that was about it.

"And my bunk-mates are great. You know we lost Renee of course. The actress? We've been wondering, is someone coming to take her bed?" Charlie glanced at her aPod.

T-Minus 4:00 (*yes!*)

Fiona, who'd slipped out earlier without a sound, returned to the barn. "I've got Greenspan on hold," she said lightly, crossing something off on her touch-screen clipboard. Charlie remembered when that clipboard belonged to her mother. Next to Charlie, it had been Bee's most valued possession.

"Oh, enough stalling, Charlie. I can't be expected to know every little thing. Now you said you had a name for me. Spit it out!"

Tick tick tick! Charlie stepped closer to Cookie and stroked the yellow fur on her neck, imploring the alpaca to help her waste a bit more of Shira's time.

"Right . . . by the way, we were wondering if you'd given any thought to holding a competition of some sort for the more musical Alphas, because a lot of the girls are kind of over the inspirational music relaxation component of lights-out. Some of these girls are so fickle. I mean, I personally *like* it just the way it is. . . ."

"Charlie! A name!" Shira was standing in front of her now, hands on her slender hips. Her Vietnamese potbellied pig squealed impatiently.

"Um, yeah. I was just getting to that."

Charlie looked down at the little blue clones, bleating away in their pen. Out of nowhere, a line of an old song her mother used to sing to her popped into her head: *Mares eat oats and does eat oats, and little lambs eat ivy. A kid will eat ivy, too, wouldn't you?* "The girl is named Lambert. Ivy Lambert. She's been spreading rumors about you, saying that the reason you wear sunglasses all the time is that your eyes are bloodshot."

"Bloodshot!" Shira unconsciously pushed her glasses up her nose. "Explain."

"She says they're bloodshot . . ." Here Charlie leaned in dramatically, lowering her voice to a whisper. "From drinking!"

Shira gasped.

"Ivy Lambert," Charlie repeated for dramatic effect. "She's got to go."

"Shira!" Fiona called. "It's time."

"Thanks for the tip," Shira muttered. Charlie the Spy had done her job, and now Shira was on to her next piece of business. "See yourself out. You don't want to be late for dinner."

"No problem." Charlie smiled. It was almost *too* easy.

0:00 (*Step two, complete.*)

As Fiona and Shira hurried away, already discussing that day's performance of Shira's portfolio on the world markets, Charlie crept around the stables until she got to the side of the house where the recycling was kept.

Her hands trembling like the feathers on Shira's baby quail, she flipped open a fuse box on the wall to reveal a keypad, praying the entry code hadn't been reset. Charlie typed in the age of each Brazille Boy—16 (Melbourne), 15 (Sydney), 14 (Darwin), 13, 13 (the twins, Taz and Dingo)—and held her breath.

"Come on, come on," she whispered, staring at the wall where she knew the panel was hidden. Besides hanging around with Darwin, she'd practically watched the place being built, and she knew it better than anyone. Hopefully, even better than Shira.

Finally! Three green LED lights flashed and a thin panel in the wall slid open to reveal a staircase to the lower level of the house, where the control room was.

She darted in, holding her breath until the door clicked shut. Charlie reasoned that she had at least three minutes until Shira ended her call, and she quickly reset her aPod's timer.

T-Minus 3:00

Pulling a pair of silver work gloves out of her skirt pocket,

Charlie raced down the stairs, heart in her throat. Not daring to turn on a light, she groped in the near-blackness toward the closet where the mainframe was kept. Inside, hundreds of tiny red, blue, and green lights blinked along the tops of dozens of connecting ports. The room was like a giant bowl of Skittles-fettuccine, crammed with thousands of wires in every color of the rainbow, draped over every nook and cranny of the closet. So much electricity happening in one place would normally look beautiful to Charlie, but now instead of seeing the wonder of technology in action, her heart sank. How on earth would she find it? She stood frozen in place, not knowing which way to turn. Her phone vibrated in her pocket, indicating two minutes had already passed.

Don't wimp out now, she told herself sternly, praying Shira's call would run long. Treating the room like a geometry problem, she reasoned the wires connected to the cameras would be closest to the bank of computers in the basement.

Gently parting a curtain of wires marked RESIDENCE, she crept toward the right-hand wall of the closet. Standing on her tiptoes, she found it: a vertical box with a neatly typed label on it marked SECURITY.

Clapping her gloved hands together, Charlie went to work. She disconnected the output wire, switching places with the input. For good measure, she typed a few system-scrambling commands into the keyboard attached to the mainframe.

Mission accomplished!

Taking the stairs two at a time, Charlie darted out of the closet, then bounded up the basement stairs as fast as her feet would take her. Sliding the panel closed again, she dashed for the side gate, thankful that the sun had dropped low in the sky. Channeling her inner Catwoman, she ran silently away from the house and hurried toward the Pavilion.

As she dashed down the walkway toward safety, the soft pink tropical twilight was suddenly drained of all its candy-colored streaks. A dreary front of gloomy slate gray quickly covered the whole island. Charlie shivered, looking up for a second before running even faster, her heart pounding in her ears.

Either Shira had just discovered that her precious cameras no longer worked, or she'd just realized that Ivy Lambert didn't exist.

5

JOAN OF ARK
MAIN DECK
TUESDAY, SEPTEMBER 21ST
7:09 P.M.

The wind whipped through Skye's white-blond waves as Taz took on more speed, throwing the boat's steering wheel to the right in a series of twists that showed off his broad shoulders and golden tan.

"I can do the circumference of the whole lake in seventeen minutes!" he yelled into the rushing wind.

"Go for it!" shouted Skye, leaning back against some rigging and feeling her hair whip around her while she squinted at the mountains surrounding the lake for signs of life. So far, so good: The only audience they had wore pine needles, not binoculars. It was a relief to be doing what she did best—basking in the attention of a cute boy. A founding member of the DSL Daters back in Westchester (they prided themselves on making super-fast connections with boys), Skye knew that hanging with a hottie on a boat was smack in the middle of her comfort zone. And now that the

50

cameras were down, Skye was free to enjoy her relapse with a serious case of Taz-Mania. When he suggested she join him for an after-dinner joyride on Shira's yacht, the *Joan of Ark*, she had jumped at the chance.

Thanks to Charlie, it was Alphas Gone Wild—just the way Skye liked it. On her way to meet Taz, Skye had passed a cluster of girls planning a midnight trip with Melbourne to hike up the mountain just past the arts building and soak in the natural hot springs. Another group was going on a late-night swim on the beach with Dingo, and the Beyoncés had teamed up with the J. K. Rowlings to create an island-wide version of capture the flag. Everyone seemed to be having fun again, but she was pretty sure she would be the talk of breakfast tomorrow if she decided to blab details of her night. After all, none of the other Alphas got a private tour around the lake—or a Brazille boy all to herself.

Taz took the boat expertly through the teal water in the center of the @-shaped island and Skye shivered, feeling the wind whip through her teeth and through the thin cotton fabric of her pearlescent white minidress, which she'd worn because it seemed nautical enough and because it made her legs look ten miles long accentuating her Clarins-assisted tan. She yanked down a pair of pale pink dance sleeves. (Thankfully, she hadn't set fire to *all* her trademark accessories—just the one pair, for symbolism's sake.) *We are so Kate and Leo right now!*

Back in Westchester, the night before Skye boarded her personal Alpha plane to Alpha Island, where magazines and TV were off-limits, she had paged through an *Us Weekly* and spotted a headline that read, "Beefcake Brazille Boy's Swift Split!" She had no idea if Taz had ever actually dated Taylor Swift, but she knew it couldn't hurt her chances that she shared the singer's long platinum wavelets, slender waist, and B-cups.

Skye pulled her Isadora Duncan long white scarf up around her blond curls and held on to the boat's railing. She had never been more sure of her decision to ditch her dance obsession and turn her attention back to what really mattered. Taz was a male version of herself, only with thick eyebrows and luscious brown-black hair—and Skye wasn't afraid to admit she loved herself.

"Look." Taz pointed to the Theater of Dionysus glinting in the sunset, suspended above the forest on the south side of the lake. "It's the dance cube!"

Skye grimaced. "I'm so over that place. Mimi hates me. No matter how hard I work, my moves are never good enough." Skye felt the familiar lump in her throat begin to form and swallowed hard, gritting her teeth through her still-raw emotions, hoping the wind in her face would dry the tears that persisted in welling up annoyingly in her eyes every time she thought about her disastrous comeback-turned-takedown.

"Forget Mimi!" Taz yelled over his shoulder. "Life's too short to do anything that isn't fun! This'll take your mind off things." His ice blue eyes twinkling mischievously, he flipped a lever that sent the *Ark* careening even faster through the water. "Wooo! Now we're rolling!"

"Mimi who?" Skye joked, but the question was sucked away by the gale-force wind, and she wasn't sure Taz heard her. Not that it mattered—she didn't want to talk about Mimi anymore. They were on a joyride, not an *oy*-ride.

As the boat swerved violently to the right, she was relieved to see that there were life preservers neatly tied to every few feet of the yacht's railing, just in case there was a disaster of *Titanic* proportions.

"I'll be right back!" she called out to him. Despite how much fun she was having and how good Taz was at taking her mind off things, she needed to go below for a bit or he would know exactly what she'd had for breakfast.

"Can you get me a Coke from the fridge downstairs?"

"One Coke coming up!" Skye salivated at the thought of high-fructose corn syrup, which was banned from the Academy cafeteria. A few slugs of liquid poison (her mother's term—Coke was also banned for all dancers at Body Alive) might make her forget all about Mimi.

She headed down a narrow stairway to the berth of the yacht and stepped into a hexagonal room decorated in a neonautical style. There was a kitchen off to one side, a sleeping area with three ovular bunk beds, and a large sitting area with two white leather couches flanking an anchor-shaped chrome coffee table.

"Must be nice," Skye said to herself, gawking at the gold wall sconces shaped like pieces of coral. She walked toward the floor-to-ceiling windows that lined the other side of the room to check out the waves they were leaving in their wake. Westchester was plenty posh, but nobody she knew back home owned a yacht like this.

"Not always," someone said.

Skye jumped, nearly toppling a futuristic pelican-shaped vase off a side table. "Who's there?" she asked the dim room.

She watched as a slender, sinewy arm reached up from one of the couches and flipped on a lamp. A second later, the head and shoulders of Sydney Brazille popped up. He'd been laying on the couch in the dark. Alone.

Weird.

"What are you doing here?" Skye hid her gritted teeth with a smile, already annoyed at the castaway for tagging along on her private date. She didn't have any classes with Sydney and he wasn't in the tabloids as much as his brothers, so she'd barely laid eyes on him before now. As she walked toward him, she was surprised by how cute he was. He wore his hair longer and tousled, and his dishwater-gray Modest Mouse T-shirt was rumpled and ripped a little at the collar, but his angular bone structure, windblown lips, and deep-set eyes that turned down at the corners made him look brooding and tragic.

"Shouldn't I be asking you that question?" He ran his hand awkwardly through his hair and raised his eyebrows at Skye.

"Taz invited me. He's upstairs, driving the boat." As if on cue, the yacht lurched to the left. Skye decided she'd better sit on the couch rather than risk breaking a lamp.

"This is where I come to write sometimes, when I need to be alone," Syd said, shutting a leather-bound notebook he'd been holding. "I thought I could get through Taz's joyride without him noticing I was down here. I've done it before." He smiled slyly, revealing a slight gap between his two front teeth.

Undeniably hawt! Skye made a mental note to tell the Jackie O's about the underappreciated charms of the most brooding of all the Brazille Boys later that night. She would never have guessed that his reputation as the shy, sensitive, soulful one wasn't pure PR hype.

"Sorry I interrupted you," said Skye. "I know how it feels to need to write stuff down. Sometimes it makes it feel more . . . real." She thought of her HAD slipper—a lot of good it had done her lately.

"You're really talented, you know," Syd said, leveling his eyes on her. It felt like he was peering into her soul.

Skye blushed as a nervous giggle escaped her lips. *How would he know?*

"I've seen you practicing in the dance cube," he went on. "After you hurt your ankle, when you had to catch up with the other dancers, I watched you practicing alone before dinner. You're awesome. You have so much soul. And heart, too." He smiled again, and Skye got another peek at the gap. "When I saw you dancing, it was like I could hear how the music sounded just from watching you."

Now she was the one who ran an awkward hand through her blond wavelets, in an attempt to cover up her bright red ears. What was she doing here? Who was this boy who watched her practice? How had she not noticed him before now?

"That's, like, the nicest thing anyone's ever said to me . . . since I got here, at least." She paused, her voice wavering slightly. "Too bad Mimi doesn't agree with you."

"She will," Syd said, locking his moss-green eyes with her turquoise blue ones. "You're too talented for her not to catch on soon."

Skye sat back and blinked at him, startled by how certain he sounded. "I thought so once, but I'm not sure now." Skye wasn't used to being so honest with someone she'd just met, but it felt good to drop her guard and let herself be vulnerable for a change. "I'm thinking of taking it down a notch. Maybe life's too short and I should just concentrate on having fun." *Like your brother says.*

"You sound like Taz," Syd replied, reading her mind. Skye blushed a deeper shade of red. "Don't let my brother and all his *fun* derail your ambition. He's never worked hard at anything. You're better than that."

Am I?

"We're docking in a minute!" Taz yelled merrily from up on deck. "I beat my record by thirty seconds!"

Syd put his finger to his lips. "I don't want Taz knowing I hang out down here," he whispered.

Syd had responded so differently to Skye's frustrations than his brother had. He really listened to her, and not just with his ears but with his heart. Like a friend and confidant. Skye had never known a guy who actually paid attention to her problems.

"Thanks for the advice. I didn't realize how much I needed it," Skye said truthfully. Just as she was starting to rethink her new plan to put fun before dancing, her aPod beeped.

SHIRA: ASSEMBLY IN FIVE MINUTES. ATTENDANCE IS MANDATORY. SOMEONE WILL BE GOING HOME.

Ohmuhgud!

Did Shira know where she was? That she had snuck onto the *Joan of Ark* with not one but *two* of her sons? Skye leapt up and spun around the room, her eyes scanning the dark mountains through the windows of the boat. *Anyone* could be watching, she realized with a shiver.

She nodded a quick good-bye to Syd, mumbling, "See you around, hopefully," as she backed away from the windows.

"Hope so." He grinned, oblivious to the deafening samba drum that had begun to beat in her temples.

Skye forced her trembling legs to carry her up the stairs of the yacht and gasped a cleansing lungful of air when she reached the deck. Taz had docked the *Ark* and was tying up the boat on a short wooden pier. In the distance, through a stand of Joshua trees, Skye could make out a few swishing metallic miniskirts as the Alphas rushed toward the Pavilion.

"Hey," he said. "You disappeared."

"Sorry," she breathed, already forgetting about Syd. "Thanks for the ride." Looking at his confident, open smile, she wondered what had kept her so long.

"Anytime." He winked. He definitely knew how cute he was.

"Your mom just called an assembly. I've gotta go," she said. Without waiting for Taz to answer, she turned around and sprinted to catch up with the other girls.

Her heart raced as her thoughts swirled faster than the water in the lake. What was intended to be a carefree escape had just confused her more than ever. Taz and Syd represented the two voices in her head: one that said to live her life for today because tomorrow would take care of itself, and the other that said to stay on track and keep working because life's passions are important.

As she ran along the path, kicking up gravel behind her with every pounding step, the two brothers blurred together like the trees flying past her. Which voice should she listen to? Which boy was the one for her?

Tragically, she might never get the chance to find out.

6

THE PAVILION
HALF-MOON THEATER
TUESDAY, SEPTEMBER 21ST
8:59 P.M.

Allie's thoughts spun and sputtered like a broken Mac-Book as ninety-nine nervous Alphas shuffled in and took their seats facing the stage in the croissant-shaped room. Every surface was shiny white, like the blank page that was her future. She blinked hard, holding back the tears that threatened to spill from her contact-lens-enhanced eyes. Someone was going home—that much had been clear from Shira's terrifying all-caps text message—and Allie was sure that someone would be her. She sat cross-legged on an egg-shaped ergonomic chair, tucking her dirty feet (how badly she wanted clean feet and a clean conscience!) under her silvery blue yoga pants. Soon, all she'd have to remember the Academy by were these pants, with the Alpha logo splashed across the butt.

She wished she could Purell this whole mess away.

One by one, the other Jackie O's arrived. As her friends

sat down next to her—*friends for just a few more minutes,
until they find out the truth!*—Allie's stomach lurched. The
Pavilion was bustling with rumors. Everywhere, girls sat in
twos and threes speculating in hushed, urgent voices about
who was going home and why. It seemed everyone thought
they were about to be on the business end of Shira's pointy-
toed pumps, but the group paranoia wasn't a comfort to
Allie. She was pretty sure nobody but her was stupid enough
to get caught masquerading as a famous multiplatinum folk
singer.

"Yo, eco-freako, you look even paler than usual. What
gives?" Triple joked, plopping down in the egg chair next to
Allie. Triple was the only Jackie O who didn't look worried
about tonight's agenda. Most of the Alphas looked sloppy,
dressed somewhere on the spectrum between pj's and safari
gear, but Triple wore her daytime school uniform. Her tawny
skin glowed with carefully applied bronzer and highlighting
powder. She had clearly dressed for the occasion—almost as
if she was excited to see one of her bunk-mates go.

"Uh . . ." Allie opened her mouth and quickly shut it,
staring imploringly out the window at a flock of purple-
bellied finches perched along the branches of a banyan tree.
Just then, clad in a flimsy dress and trailing a long white
scarf that Allie was sure was not regulation Alphas, Skye
collapsed gracefully into the seat on Allie's other side.

"Say good-bye to Skye Hamilton, girls," squeak-sighed

Skye, waving one end of her scarf dramatically in a gesture of *bon voyage*. "I'm about to go down in flames."

"Why *you?*" Triple looked like she was struggling to choke down a smile. Allie made a mental reminder not to trust Triple—she was faker than a thirty-dollar Gucci clutch.

"I met Taz for a joyride around the lake on Shira's boat. Obviously she must have found out, and voilà"—Skye snapped her pink-polished fingers—"here we are." She craned her neck toward the back of the room to see if any of the boys had bothered showing up.

"Dumb da-dumb dumb," replied Triple, rolling her eyes.

"You're safe, Skye—the cameras are still off. And that's why *I'm* going home," said Charlie, plopping down next to Skye with a defeated thud. "Not to mention the fake name I gave her. I'll text you from Hoboken."

Just then, Allie saw Darwin slip in through a side door and find a seat toward the back of the room. Her brain did a backflip, taking her to that night last week in the subterranean tunnels under the vertical farm, where they had shared an unbelievable first kiss. Her insides fizz-melted like a root beer float. *Darwin's cinnamon-flavored lips on mine! The song he wrote about me!*

Allie thought her heart might explode as she locked eyes with him over the heads of fifty Alpha girls. The eye embrace lasted a heart-pumping three-Mississippis, until Darwin finally broke away. A second later, Allie's phone beeped.

Darwin: If cameras are still down after this, meet me at the entrance to the tunnel. I miss you.

Allie couldn't resist him any longer. She'd stayed away for two whole weeks, but on the slim chance she survived Shira's assembly, her Darwin moratorium would be officially put to rest. Darwin wanted it, Charlie wanted it, and Allie *desperately* wanted it. She just wished she could warn him about what might be coming. But how do you tell someone you're not who they think you are without sounding like a fake? Because there was nothing false about her feelings for Darwin.

Allie: I'll be there, if your mom doesn't send me home tonight.

She paused, trying to think of how to tell him that the real Allie—not the imposter version—missed him. She brought her fingers back to her keypad and typed.

Allie: You make me feel like myself.

Suddenly, the whole Pavilion sounded like it had been dropped into a popcorn machine. Overhead, the sky went from slate gray to stormy, and hailstones the size of golf balls angrily pelted the glass skylights. Ninety-nine Alphas and

Darwin all went instantly silent, watching the storm and waiting for Shira to arrive. The island had been built inside its own biosphere, with Shira at its helm. When she was hot under the collar, the island compensated by cooling off—the weather was more or less entirely dictated by her moods.

"She's pissed," whispered Charlie. "And she's almost here."

The crowd was nervous and mute as they waited for Shira to take the stage. Allie half expected a panel of judges to show up, or at least some *Survivor*-style torches. It was clear that heads were about to roll.

Shira's words from last week in her office thundered in Allie's skull:

Identity theft . . . illegal . . . tell everyone . . .

But what she'd written to Darwin was true; she *was* herself here—a new kind of self, one who took risks, who was brave and adventurous—whenever she wasn't busy worrying about being Allie J.

Allie wanted to write him one more text, but the insistent tapping of a manicured finger against a microphone signaled Shira's arrival at the Pavilion. A hush fell over the girls as Shira walked out onto the stage, her dark glasses reflecting the recessed stage lights. With her wild auburn waves and long black maxidress, she reminded Allie of the zombies from Michael Jackson's "Thriller" video.

At the thought of what was surely coming next, Allie's empty stomach fluttered like the school of angelfish she'd seen last week in the tunnels with Darwin. The Jackie O's would hate her forever. Darwin would toss her aside like yesterday's homework. The song he'd written for her would curdle like old milk, along with the night they'd had together and their amazing kiss. Another Alpha—*probably the real Allie J!*—would soon capture his heart forever.

And Allie would have to slink home in disgrace. She couldn't decide which fate was more hideous: being sent to juvie for identity theft or having to endure the sight of Fletcher and Trina with no possibility of escape until college.

A smile played on Shira's lips, thin and lethal as a razorblade.

Ohmuhgud, my life is over.

"This is it," she heard Charlie mumble.

Allie put her hand over Charlie's and squeezed. "You'll be fine," she murmured. She wished more than anything that they both would.

Shira paced back and forth across the stage until the silence that blanketed the crowd of Alphas went from expectant to terrified. The hailstorm died out as quickly as it had started, and now it was quiet enough for Allie to hear her heart thundering in her ears.

"G'day, my lollies. Daphne Sacks. Chloe Merrill. Devendra Banks. Hazel Vellieux. Mallory Rice. Robin

Nicoletti. Naomi Shultz. Elizabeth Sanders-Post. Jessie-Lynn Jones. Lauren Flowers. Isobel Abeles. Ivy Lambert. If I called your name, please stand up."

Eleven pale, terrified girls rose slowly from their seats, wringing their hands like finalists in a perverse pageant.

"You are hereby dismissed from Alpha Academy, effective immediately. Your teachers have reported that you are not Alpha material."

A wave of relief swelled among the remaining Alphas as the executed eleven shuffled tearily out of the room. Allie, Skye, and Charlie stood up in a spontaneous three-girl hug—miraculously, they had dodged another round of Shira's bullets!

As the room buzzed with girls trying to figure out why the executed eleven had been cut, Allie looked over her shoulder at Darwin, still standing in the back corner. He winked. Allie grinned back. *Uhmuhgud, am I really safe?* Allie would keep posing as Allie J for the next four years if it meant tasting Darwin's cinnamon-flavored lips again. Sure, there would be a lot more Purell and pumice stones for her feet, but . . .

"Uh-oh," Charlie whispered, interrupting Allie's mental happy-dance. "There's more. She's got another bombshell. That's her bombshell smile."

Sure enough, Allie could see Shira's lips twitching like the whiskers of a cat.

"And now," Shira's Aussie-inflected voice boomed, "a little something to celebrate another day at the most prestigious school on earth. Those of you who work hard—who are *true to yourselves* like the women for whom your houses are named—will rise to the top, not just here but in the real world. And speaking of the real world, it's time for a show!"

A curtain on the stage went up, revealing an electric guitar, a microphone, and three backup musicians. All that was missing was . . . *Ohmuhgud ohmuhgud ohmuhgud.*

Allie's posture hermit-crabbed as she tried to shrink into her egg-chair. All the pieces were falling into place. Shira wanted maximum humiliation, maximum effect. Allie watched Shira's lips move in slo-mo as the full terror of what was happening sank in.

"Allie J will now sing her hit song 'I'm a Fuel for Your Love'! Come on up, Allie!"

Charlie beamed at Allie. "You didn't tell us you were performing!"

"Go, girl, enjoy it," said Skye.

Ohmuhgud Ohmuhgud! My social homicide has officially arrived! Allie had the silent, ridiculous smile of a demented mime plastered on her parched lips. She stood up and nearly fell over on legs as supportive as JELL-O.

She wobbled slowly toward the stage in a delirious fog, squeezing her hands together in a futile attempt to keep them from shaking. *Trigger pulled.*

Eighty-seven Alphas cheered her on as she climbed onto the stage and took the guitar from Shira's outstretched arms. She had memorized all the words to Allie J's songs, but all the lyrics in the world couldn't give her a good singing voice. Even worse, she hadn't touched a guitar in her life, other than one unfortunate incident at age ten when she had won a backstage pass to a Justin Timberlake concert. Allie began to shake. Panic pressed down on her like a 300-pound elephant sitting on her chest.

"I've been looking forward to this all week," Shira said, leaning in and speaking in low tones over the applause.

Allie walked toward the mic, praying for a miracle. She could barely see or breathe, and she didn't know whether she was about to cry or hurl. A snotty, blubbering, full-blown sob-fest loomed in her throat and her vision had gone fuzzy from fear. She looked up at Darwin through a curtain of tears and saw his blurred form in the back row, clapping wildly, his gorgeous face sporting a proud grin for the girl she was pretending to be.

As Allie reached for the guitar, a panel began to open up in the center of the stage floor. From the hole in the floor came the first few familiar notes of "I'm a Fuel for Your Love."

And playing them was the real Allie J. Guitar in hand, wearing a tattered white dress and a dozen dangly necklaces, smiling and confident—with a real mole.

As the audience gasped, every part of Allie remained frozen onstage except for the fat, mascara-tinted tears that rolled down her cheeks. Here at last was the real thing, the one with all the talent and fame, the girl she'd been pretending to be, easily stepping (barefoot, with a minimal carbon footprint, but still!) into a life that was now Allie A's.

Just a few feet away, Allie J began to sing:

Without you I am cold
A chin without a goatee
So if the truth be told
I need you to ignite me

The audience looked from fake-Allie to real-Allie and murmured confusedly to one another. Then most of them jumped to their feet and started to dance, deciding, Allie guessed, to enjoy themselves and figure out what was wrong with this picture later. Allie J continued her throaty performance:

This is where I'm torn
You're bad energy
Now I fill up on corn
It's all about synergy

Allie A couldn't move. Her legs were stuck to the stage floor like they'd been glued there. Never in her life had she felt this humiliated. The time she tripped while working as a mall model, busting open her lip and bleeding all over the clothes, didn't even come close. Fletcher and Trina's betrayal was a cakewalk compared to this. She closed her eyes in a futile attempt to block out the circus-mirror effect her mortification was having on the room. But even behind closed eyes, Allie saw the sneers on every pretty Alpha face.

Take a hint
You're totally done
Reduce the carbon footprint
It's best for everyone

As Allie J played the final bridge of the song, Allie A opened her eyes and searched out the Jackie O's. They hadn't stood up for the performance. They paid no attention to the real Allie J, focusing only on Allie, their eyes flashing with shock . . . then rage. What was worse, behind the seething anger, each of them looked hurt. Especially Charlie. Allie swallowed—her throat felt like Brillo. The pain she had caused her friends was ten times scarier to contemplate than their anger.

I acted like a fool
Before I knew better

Don't pump me full of fuel
Don't dry-clean my hemp sweater

Finally Allie's eyes found Darwin in the back row. He stared straight ahead, not willing to even make eye contact with her. The look on his face was stony and furious and devastatingly sad.

As the last bars of Allie J's song faded out, Shira stepped back onto the stage, clapping her hands along with the rest of the audience. Everyone but the Jackie O's and Darwin hollered and whistled.

"Allie J. Abbott, everyone! Let's give her another big round of applause, shall we?" As the clapping died out, Shira crossed the stage and rested a manicured hand on Allie's shoulder. "And, of course, you've already met Allie A. Abbott."

Allie willed herself not to flinch at Shira's icy touch.

"Whose talent, up until today, has been impersonating a folk singer. Let's hope Ms. Abbott finds her real talent soon, or she'll be leaving us like our twelve friends tonight. Assembly dismissed." Shira flounced offstage, leaving the two Allies—one drinking in the adoration of a quickly forming crowd of girls, the other standing alone, wishing she could morph into a hologram and vanish into thin air.

Fresh tears sprang into Allie's eyes as Darwin flipped up the hood of his sweatshirt and stormed out of the room without even glancing her way. Her gaze moved to the Jackie O's, who lingered in their chairs, talking in hushed voices. Through her tears, they looked streaky and blurred like a Van Gogh.

Each of them glared at her with a mixture of hurt, anger, and pity. They seemed embarrassed, too: maybe a little bit for Allie, but also for themselves, for having believed her lies.

Allie shivered in the dark shadow she'd cast over the Jackie O's. Her lie had seemed so insignificant in her bedroom in Santa Ana—what was one little initial?—but with time it had grown bigger than Godzilla. Yet now she felt smaller than a grain of sand. She shrank into herself even more as she watched Charlie and Skye stand up and walk out of the room together arm in arm, brushing silently past Alphas trying to milk them for information about how Allie could have gotten away with this.

The Oprahs to Allie's right and the Michelle Obamas to her left were whispering and laughing, and every few seconds she heard the beep of an aPod as the Alphas processed the scandal via text. Out of the remaining eighty-seven girls, only Allie J looked at her with a neutral expression.

"I'm, like, so flattered by how much you wanted to be me," she said over the throng of Alphas that surrounded her.

Her aPod beeped, and Allie's insides clenched in anticipation.

The sender was anonymous.

Q: How many Allie J's does it take to change a lightbulb?
A: Three: One to change it, one to write a song about it, and one imposter to take all the credit.

Allie turned off her phone and took a long, shaky breath, wondering what would become of her now. She couldn't go home, not after Shira had given her a second chance. But how could she possibly stay here?

As her tear-filled eyes traveled from one disdainful face to another, Allie felt like nuclear waste. Unwanted, untouchable, and ugly.

If this was what Shira meant by facing the music, Allie never wanted to hear this song again.

7

THE PAVILION
GREAT LAWN
TUESDAY, SEPTEMBER 21ST
10:36 P.M.

"I can't believe this!" Skye fumed. "I thought we could trust her."

She and Charlie had joined the stampede of Alphas spilling out onto the lawn in front of the Pavilion, and Skye had begun to twirl back and forth between two planters filled with wildflowers, processing Allie's shocking revelation with her limbs as much as with her brain.

Charlie sighed, feeling a little dizzy from watching Skye. "I thought I was really getting to know her. What a joke."

"I mean, it's one thing to lie about little things, like someone's outfit not making them look fat or someone's boyfriend not being a potential contestant on *Beauty and the Geek*. But this! This is *beyond*. This is *sick*." Skye stopped spinning and stared straight into Charlie's red-rimmed eyes. Both of them had shed a few bitter tears in the auditorium during Allie's unmasking.

Charlie looked past the milling throng of Alphas and spotted Darwin standing in the shadows of a palm grove just on the outskirts of the patio. He was staring up at something, apparently studying a bunch of coconuts. Just then, Allie burst through the Pavilion doors and ran past Skye and Charlie, flinching as if she thought they might hit her. Her path was arrow straight, her target Darwin.

"That's gonna get ugly," muttered Charlie. If there was one thing she knew, it was that nothing made Darwin angrier than being lied to. She thought back to the week they spent in Alexandria, Egypt, two years ago. Shira was doing a special on Cleopatra as the first feminist, and everywhere Shira went, they followed. Charlie and Syd had punked Darwin, wrapping Mel in bandages and having him pop up from behind a tomb in one of the pyramids. When he'd found out Charlie was involved, he'd looked into her eyes and asked her never to lie to him again. "Some guys are cool with less than one hundred percent honesty," he'd said. "I'm not one of them."

Charlie's stomach gurgled with guilt. She had promised she would never lie to him again, and look at her now. Darwin had no idea that she'd traded their relationship for the chance to share the same high school. And as if that weren't bad enough, she'd encouraged him to be with a girl who made *The Hills* look like *PBS NewsHour*.

Allie was in front of him now, trying to embrace him in

the shadows of the palm trees, but Darwin shook her off. His face twisted in a mask of anger and hurt; Darwin waved his hand in the direction of Shira's compound. The other hand pointed emphatically in the direction of the dorms. A few seconds later, Allie backed away from him and ran toward the beach, looking like Shakespeare's Juliet moments before desperately drinking poison.

I know that feeling. Charlie shuddered, remembering the soul-ripping sensation of ending things with Darwin.

As Allie disappeared down the pebble path toward the dorms and Skye began to launch into another rant about liars, schemers, and poseurs throughout history, Charlie's aPod beeped.

SHIRA: I NEED TO SEE YOU ASAP. TAKE THE TRAIN TO THE RESIDENCE.

What now? Charlie stood staring down at her phone, the now-familiar sensation of Shira-phobia constricting her lungs. Was she getting busted after all?

Ping!

SHIRA: NOW!

Alpha Island's translucent train hissed to a vibrating halt in front of her. Everyone called it the bubble train, since it looked like a giant string of Marge Simpson–style pearls, a line of bubble compartments connected by thin white tubes. The door to a car whooshed open and a recording of Bee's soothing British voice said, "Welcome aboard, Charlie."

Thanks, Mom, Charlie thought-answered back. *Wish you were here.*

"You. Of course. Perfect."

Charlie jumped, slamming her head against the top of the door frame in surprise. Darwin was slouched in the corner of the car, looking at Charlie like she was a plate of food left out overnight—definitely gross, possibly salmonella spreading. A cinnamon-scented toothpick dangled from his pursed lips.

"Ouch!" Charlie rubbed her head. "You scared me!"

"Whoops," muttered Darwin, staring out the window at the line of Joshua trees on the other side of the train.

"I'm not following you," Charlie said, doing her best to ignore his tone. She clambered aboard before the train left without her. "Your mom wants to see me."

The only place to sit was next to Darwin, and Charlie pressed herself against the wall of the car to make sure there was an inch of empty space between them. Before their breakup, the seat would have seemed too big for them. Now, the heat vibrating off his body felt like a warning.

As the train snaked through the campus, the short ride began to feel like an eternity. A pang of longing shot through Charlie, but she took a deep breath and mentally slapped it down. Would there ever be a time when seeing Darwin wouldn't make her wonder how she could have given him up?

"I don't trust one single girl on this island. You're all trustbusters. Faking your identities, spying for my mom . . ." He trailed off, looking out the window at the tangled forest, as impenetrable as the barrier between them.

"I'm not actually spying for your mom," she snapped, taking his poisonous bait. "I can't believe you would actually think that."

"I don't know what to believe anymore," he said, pulling out his phone and examining the time.

Charlie clamped her mouth shut and sat on her hands, worried that if she lost track of them she would try to touch his shoulder or run her fingers over the floppy light brown waves of his hair. She couldn't nurse him through Allie's betrayal, not when she'd worked so hard to help the two of them get together. And even though she wanted to tell him the truth about everything, about the breakup, about Shira forcing it on her in exchange for allowing her the chance to become an Alpha, she knew she couldn't. She made a silent pledge to herself: From now on, the only Brazille she was going to kiss was Shira's butt. Otherwise, what was the point of any of this?

Just then, the bubble train doors whooshed open and

Bee's voice announced their destination. *Wish me luck, Mom.* Charlie followed Darwin up the walkway to the back entrance, a sliding glass door that led into the kitchen. She stared dejectedly at the backs of his blue Converse, worn thin at the heels. He slid the door open so roughly she thought for a second it might slide off its hinges and shatter into a million pieces, but it stayed on its track.

Just like I'm going to do.

Charlie walked into the kitchen and waited there uncertainly. She wasn't about to follow Darwin, who ran upstairs without even saying good-bye.

8

Sacrificing her beauty sleep for boys, Skye lifted up the comforter she was hiding under in order to get some air and to make sure the sound of her thumbs furiously tapping the keyboard of her aPod hadn't woken anyone. Charlie was gone, and Allie's bed was still empty. After the assembly and her humiliating public breakup with Darwin, Allie hadn't bothered to come back to Jackie O. Skye wondered if she *ever* would. People could survive on tropical islands by catching fish and sleeping in caves. After what Allie had already pulled off, anything seemed possible. Then again, maybe Allie was somewhere begging Shira to be sent home. Skye didn't know which was worse: going home defeated or staying here and being hated.

To Skye's left, Triple Threat drooled on her pillow, enjoying the infuriatingly deep sleep of the guiltless and the shallow. Skye could detect a half smile twitching intermittently

80

on Triple's lips. And next to Triple lay the newest member of the Jackie O house.

The real Allie J.

To avoid any more confusion between herself and Allie the Imposter, she had asked that everyone call her AJ. She sung-snored in her sleep, her small, pale frame splayed out diagonally on her canopied bed. Skye narrowed her aquamarine eyes and studied AJ's face. She couldn't decide if the sing-snoring was cute or annoying.

Not my problem, she reminded herself, swiveling her head back and forth until her vertebrae popped. She needed to keep her friends close, her enemies closer, and the boys right where she wanted them—in the palm of her hand.

Grinning, she dove back under her comforter to continue her text-a-thon with Taz and Syd. If Vegas knew how well she juggled boys, she'd be asked to star in Cirque du Soleil. Neither brother knew about the other, and Skye planned to keep it that way.

Skye: I have some questions. R U ready?
Taz: Bring it awn!
Syd: I'm an open book.

Skye wished she had some friends around to figure out which Brazille was "the one." But in the absence of besties, she had come up with a questionnaire to help her decide.

It was like a text-only version of that old show *The Dating Game*, only without the seventies' feathered haircuts and campy theme music.

Q: Which flavor of ice cream describes you best?

Taz: Nutty Coconut

Syd: Passion Fruit

Skye: Berry Berry Extraordinary

Q: What popular TV show title best describes your life?

Taz: The Young and the Restless

Syd: Family Guy

Skye: Lost

Q: Name three things you would take with you to a deserted island.

Taz: Fifty friends, an amazing stereo system, and a fully stocked yacht!

Syd: A notebook, a pen, and you.

Skye: Music and someone to dance with. And lip gloss. ☺

Q: What's the craziest thing you ever did?

Taz: Skateboarded for twenty minutes on the Great Wall of China before I got arrested by the Chinese police.

Syd: I rewrote the end of one of Salman Rushdie's novels and sent it to him. He wrote back and said he liked it. . . .

Skye: Coming to Alpha Academy!

Q: What's your favorite quality in a girl?

Taz: Spontaneity

Syd: Passion

Skye: Loyalty

Q: What's your favorite quality in a guy?

Taz: Adventurousness

Syd: Humility

Skye: Hotness? Kidding!

Q: If you had $100 to spend on our date, how would you spend it?

Taz: Trapeze lessons.

Syd: I'd hand it to you and watch you spend it.

Skye: An underground dance troupe performance followed by an after party somewhere exclusive!

Q: What celeb do people say you look like?

Taz: Robert Pattinson!

Syd: I'm an original.

Skye: Taylor Swift. It's the hair.

Q: Least favorite quality in a girl?

Taz: Shyness

Syd: Apathy

Skye: Fakeness

Q: Biggest fear?

Taz: Death

Syd: Public speaking

Skye: Not making it as a dancer. And your mom!

Q: Where do you see yourself in ten years?

Taz: Breaking the world record for motorcycling across the continent of Africa, running a multibillion-dollar corporation, and throwing great parties with the girl of my dreams.

Syd: Winning the Pulitzer Prize for my novel and running a nonprofit dedicated to promoting world peace.

Skye: I don't even know where I see myself in ten minutes.

As the texts accumulated, Skye's aPod went from pleasantly warm to hazardously hot and her heart followed suit. First she was confused, but now she was positively flummoxed. Which Brazille brother was right for her? Choosing between them was like flipping channels between *The Hills* and *Gossip Girl*, like being asked to dance by Fred Astaire and Mikhail Baryshnikov simultaneously. She wanted them both, just not at the same time! The two brothers appealed to the two sides of her personality: Taz was the ultimate party guy, the guy all the girls wanted, the one that would make Skye feel glamorous, popular, and like her life was one long adventure, full of risk and packed with fun. Syd was passionate, devoted, and romantic. He had watched all of Skye's dance videos on YouTube and told Skye he was mesmerized by the way she made the routines her own. He made her feel like a misunderstood genius, like she shouldn't give up on her dream because quitting dance would deprive the world of something it needed.

Skye couldn't decide who was right or which Skye was the real her. Her inner devil and her inner angel were at war, and right now she wasn't sure who was winning. How to choose the better boyfriend? Skye suddenly longed to sit across from her mother in their Westchester kitchen, hashing it out over steaming cups of tea and a plate of butter cookies. Once the prima ballerina for the Bolshoi Ballet, Natasha Flailenkoff had had more boys after her than Megan Fox. But Skye's mother was nearly three thousand miles away.

Skye sighed, turning on her side to do a few pilates leg lifts for inspiration. The *Dating Game* comparison quiz wasn't conclusive enough for such a huge decision. And even two real dates wouldn't help, since Skye forgot all about one boy when she was with the other. If only there was a way to get everyone in the same room at the same time. . . . *Aha!* Skye paused mid–leg lift, her right toe pointed toward the Little Dipper. That was it!

She cracked her thumb knuckles and typed.

Skye: Party @ the dance studio Wednesday nite after lights-out. You in?
Taz: In there like swimwear!
Syd: Can't wait to see you dance in person.

Yay! Skye loved her idea, and she loved that they loved it. Friday night, she would take advantage of the broken cameras and create fun from thin air, starring as the hostess with the most-ess and taking her pick between two hotties. *Let the best Brazille win.* She smiled, signing off with a good-night air kiss for both.

She stuck her aPod in its charging dock and curled up in bed, flexing and bending her tired fingers. The stars twinkled at her through the curved glass ceiling above her bed, and the even breathing of her bunk-mates now seemed peaceful instead of irritating. The last thing she saw before closing her eyes was Natasha's HAD slipper, gleaming in the moonlight like a secret promise.

Skye reached toward her nightstand and fingered the frayed satin edge of the lavender toe shoe. Maybe it couldn't bring her success in dance, but at least it might help her snag a boyfriend.

Let Triple be the ballerina bun-head, Skye thought as she let herself drift off. The only buns she was interested in right now belonged to Taz and Syd.

9

"Charlie!" Shira whispered in an uncharacteristically frantic tone. "Is that you?"

Charlie's stomach sank as she looked around, trying to source the location of Shira's voice. She saw immaculate Italian marble countertops, two ovens large enough to roast a pig in, and a spotless stainless steel fridge.

"Shira?" she called.

"In here!" a voice called from behind the narrow door to the pantry. A veiny hand wearing Shira's Australian opal cocktail ring reached out from the crack in the door and motioned her in.

A sliver of light fell over Shira's face, and it had panic written all over it. "I'm telling you this with the expectation of the utmost secrecy, Charlie. The cameras are down. They have been down for hours. I've been on the phone with Steve Jobs, with Bill Gates, with CompuServe, and the president of Geek Squad." As Shira talked, Charlie studied the stacks of cans behind her: Vegemite, Marmite, Nutella, tuna belly, lychee nuts, mandarin orange segments, Vienna sausages, Spam, water chestnuts, caviar, pickled plums—Shira's household could survive for at least a year solely on international oddities and fifties throwbacks.

"No one can help me over the phone, and it seems they're all currently aiding the CIA with a potential national disaster. Therefore—" Shira paused, sounding extremely put out. Charlie brought her focus from the Marmite back to Shira's face.

"There*fore*, Chah-lie. Your eyes and ears are needed, Lolly. Now more than ever. I need to be informed of who obeys the rules of the Academy and who does not. *Capice?*"

"Okay, but—"

"God, I'm in need of a *mass*age. I gave Jorge the week off, and my neck is so tight, Charlie, you cannot imagine the stress."

You're stressed?!? Charlie wanted to scream, clenching her jaw. *Try living through what you've forced me into!* All of Charlie's loneliness, all of her lies—*everything* was the fault of the woman cowering before her in the pantry. Her mother leaving for England and giving up the job that sustained her for thirteen years? Shira's fault. Charlie having to choose between dumping Darwin or moving three thousand miles away from him? Shira's fault. And now things had gotten so twisted that Charlie had risked everything to help her friend (who was a total fake) get together with her ex (who, if she went by today, was now a total jerk). Her head was about to *explode* from the stress.

But Charlie gritted her teeth and swallowed her rage. The new Charlie wasn't going to let opportunities to impress the Brazille nut slide by anymore. She'd given up too much already.

"I can fix it," she said.

"You know a good masseuse?" asked Shira, rubbing her neck and whimpering like a kicked puppy.

"No, I can fix the computer system." *If I figured out how to break it, surely I can fix it. . . .*

Shira snort-laughed, picking up a jar of Vegemite and examining its nutrition label. "Aren't you adorable, Charlie. There's a difference between making nail polish and fixing the most sophisticated camera system on the planet. I hardly think someone like you would know the first thing about it."

Someone like me built it!

"Give me a chance," Charlie said. "I might surprise you."

And impress you.

"Fine," sighed Shira, opening the Vegemite. "I suppose you can't make things any worse."

Charlie headed for the basement, and Shira trailed behind her.

"How do you know where the system is housed? I don't recall telling you." Shira glared at Charlie suspiciously as she swallowed a mouthful of crackers.

"Um, well . . . actually," Charlie stalled, looking up at the crystal chandelier hanging in Shira's hallway. *Stupid!* How could she have been so careless? "My mom . . ."

"Your mum?" Shira purred sarcastically.

Shira's Vegemite-scented breath ticked her pores. She clutched frantically at the recesses of her brain. Suddenly, an excuse sprouted up like a weed from the mud.

"My mom, yeah. She kept the blueprints tacked up in our living room while this place was being built. Guess I absorbed them without even trying?" Charlie flashed a relieved smile.

"Quite perceptive." Shira's voice was disappointed but appeased. "Off you go, then."

Charlie headed down the basement stairs, and the only peep out of Shira now was the rustling of cracker casing.

Realizing she needed to slip into the mainframe closet to reattach the disconnected wires, Charlie cleared her throat. She needed to distract Shira somehow.

"Oh, shoot."

"What?" came the voice at the top of the stairs.

"I need to do a total restart. It requires a paper clip." Charlie cocked her head at Shira, hoping she would take the hint.

"Oh, blimey. All right, I'll get one."

As soon as Shira disappeared from the top of the stairs, Charlie slipped into the mainframe closet and switched the two wires back. She quickly crept out and was back in her original seat when Shira came down with the paper clip. Now all she'd have to do was a few simple computer commands, and Shira would think she was a genius.

Charlie sat at a desk chair in front of a massive bank of computers just outside the network closet doors, all of which worked fine, except for the monitors that were supposed to be beaming pictures from around campus. Those were all black. She flipped a bunch of switches, faking her way along so Shira wouldn't realize she'd been the one to break the system. Finally, after enough time had passed, Charlie began trying to repair the code she'd deliberately scrambled yesterday. She typed in a series of commands and repaired the strings of ALPHA-SQL sequencing she'd disturbed, keeping her toes crossed since her fingers were busy. She held her breath and pushed the ENTER key, practically tasting the victory in saving Shira's precious cameras and finally proving herself as a tech whiz.

"Incorrect sequence! Shutting down in fifteen seconds," the computer's voice calmly informed her, followed by three loud *bleeps*.

"No!" Charlie leaned over and banged her forehead against the table, groaning quietly. Why was fixing something so much harder than breaking it? And why was that true for hearts as well as hard drives?

After everything that had happened in the last three weeks—ending things with Darwin, sending her mom home, losing the first friend she'd made on the island, and faking a blackout—Charlie was beginning to think she was better at breaking things than making them.

10

Sprawled out on a white foam chaise longue, Allie reached up to wipe a drop of morning dew from her cheek.

"Ew! Ohmuhgud!"

This was not dew. It was thick and grainy. Worst of all, it was warm! Allie staggered up from her makeshift bed. *Bird poop!* She clawed furiously at her face, every cell in her germophobe heart screaming out in self-pity. But Allie was too tired to cry over this latest indignity. Besides, her tear ducts were drained dry from too much crying.

"Stupid nature!" Allie grumbled, her throat coated in phlegmy gunk and her eyes crusty and swollen. She'd spent the night sleeping al fresco, curled up under a towel on the back porch of the Jackie O house. Nature had been up for hours: As the island came to life under a Creamsicle-orange sunrise, Allie had been tortured by screeching mynah birds, cooing quail, chattering monkeys, and a horrible insect intent on dive-bombing her ears.

"I'm up! You win!" Now that her eyes were open in puffy slits, it was only a matter of time before she had to face her new life. If she looked half as beat-up as she felt, it was going to be the longest day on earth.

She took a deep, shaky breath and tried to summon the courage to open the sliding glass door to the Jackie O house, where soap and Purell waited like old friends. Her only friends, actually, since everyone else was either not speaking to her or coming up with clever rap lyrics for a song called "Imposter Allie" that was making the rounds among the Alphas.

Last night, she'd been too ashamed to face her bunkmates, too devastated after her confrontation with Darwin outside the Pavilion to defend herself to them. Darwin didn't want anything to do with her ever again, and she was pretty sure the Jackie O's felt the same way.

As Allie furiously wiped her face with her hand, the sliding glass door of the Jackie O house slid open. Thalia, their house muse, stepped out, wearing a silky yellow robe and holding a steaming mug in her enormous hands. A former point guard for her college basketball team, Thalia had turned to her psychology major after a knee injury sidelined her b-ball career. Since she couldn't live her dream, she helped others live theirs.

"Hi Thalia." Allie drew in a shaky breath and straightened her slumped shoulders.

"Hi Allie. I thought you could use some tea." Thalia passed her the mug. "It's got milk thistle and chamomile in it, both of which have calming properties."

"Thanks," said Allie, rubbing her poo-hand on her yoga pants. Fresh tears welled up in her eyes over Thalia's kindness. She wondered how she could possibly have any more water in her body after all the crying she'd done last night.

"Waste not fresh tears over old griefs, Allie. Euripides," Thalia said softly, sitting down next to Allie on the edge of the chaise.

Allie took a dejected sip from her mug and stared out at the tangle of trees, their branches home to dozens of yellow-bellied finches. She wished she could be as carefree as those stupid birds.

"People will forget. They'll move on, and you'll start over. Mary Pickford once said, 'You may have a fresh start any moment you choose, for this thing we call "failure" is not the falling down, but the staying down.'"

Allie nodded slowly, blinking as she examined Thalia's pretty, poreless face. Allie had been down so long, she wasn't sure she would recognize "up" if it landed on her like that pile of bird poop.

Thalia continued to fill the silence with her relentless optimism. "There is a reason you're still here. Sh faith in you. If she didn't, she would have sent you home. Everything will feel more manageable after you head inside and face the music."

Would everyone please stop using that corny expression?

Allie blinked back her tears and rubbed her aching eyes. Her contacts felt like tiny circles of sandpaper. Trying to embrace the bright side of her miserable situation, she plucked them out and threw them into the bushes. "I guess I don't need these green lenses anymore." The gravelly sound of her voice surprised her. How many hours had it been since she'd spoken a word to anyone?

"Good, that's a positive step forward." Thalia beamed. "The Greek philosopher Thucydides said, 'The secret of Happiness is Freedom, and the secret of Freedom, Courage.' You have the chance to find all of that now."

Allie shrugged. Actually, throwing away her lenses did feel kind of freeing. Now her navy blue eyes would be free to shine again. And someday, her dull, dyed black-brown hair would grow out and her sandy-blond mane would return. Allie was voted best tressed two years in a row in junior high, after all. And now she could finally stop worrying about that dumb "mole" on her upper lip; no more sleeping exclusively on her left side for fear of smudges! Thalia was right—Allie would only be happy once she was free.

Free to be herself, to stop acting like she knew what a carbon footprint was. Free to wear shoes! To Purell a hundred times a day if she wanted! Free to quote her favorite lines from Katherine Heigl rom-coms. Free to wear makeup and eat meat and keep up with celebrity gossip. She could stop pretending she cared about the earth and focus on the stars.

But if she were so free, why did she still feel so trapped?

"Go on," said Thalia, motioning toward the open door.

Allie nodded, summoning her courage. She swallowed hard and stood up, putting one bare foot in front of the other. "Okay," she said in a tiny voice.

Her heart clanging like a firehouse bell, Allie stepped into the climate-controlled study lounge. She placed her palm on the "SnakScan" touch-screen snack dispenser and waited as the machine performed a bio-analysis to determine what she should eat. Expecting a packet of kale chips or a PowerBar, Allie smiled when the Plexiglas slot in the wall popped open and offered her a little yellow bag of peanut M&M's.

Allie ripped open a corner of the bag and poured the M&M's into her mouth, chewing furiously in an attempt to quiet her growling stomach.

She slowly climbed the clear spiral staircase to the bedroom, stuffing her hands in the pockets of her yoga pants to hide their shaking. Stepping into the snow-globe-shaped dome, she flinched, expecting the Jackie O's to throw things at her—shoes, pillows, insults, *something*.

But when she walked in, nobody even looked up. The girls were all sprawled on Renee's old bed, crowded around its new occupant.

The real Allie J.

Ohmuhgud.

"And, you know, when Shira told me what was going on here in my name, I mean, I knew I had to come and set the record straight. I just felt so *violated*, you know? Like a snake being forced to molt before her time, just for someone's ugly snakeskin shoes! Which is just so ironic, because I don't even *wear* shoes, you know?"

Triple, Skye, and Charlie each nodded sympathetically, as if Allie J had actually been traumatized by the experience of meeting Allie A.

"You handled it really well, AJ. I don't think I would have been as nice about it if it were me," said Skye, wrapping her white-blond waves into a bun and stabbing a pen through it to keep the hair in place.

She's AJ now?

Everyone stood up, still pointedly ignoring Allie, and began getting ready for the day. They all vanished into the bathroom or the study lounge. Allie was alone again with the whole bedroom all to herself. She walked over to her bed and wasn't surprised to find it roped off with metallic Alpha-issue scarves. Hanging from them was a sign:

CRIME SCENE—IDENTITY-THEFT ZONE

A chalk outline of Allie J and her guitar had been traced on the ground at the foot of Allie's bed. *What was it Thalia said about courage?*

Allie's aPod beeped in her pocket and she pulled out the gold device. An envelope with an A seal opened on the screen, and a virtual form letter slid out, followed by a schedule.

Dear Allie A. Abbott: Our records indicate that you have not yet declared an area of concentration. As such, your course schedule has expanded to include more offerings. Failure to choose an ALPHA track by the end of the semester will lead to expulsion.

Allie's stomach lurched at the word *expulsion*. She scrolled through her new class schedule and felt more exhausted than ever.

Time	Class	Location
7:30 a.m.	BREAKFAST AND MOTIVATIONAL LECTURE Every day you will receive a lecture from a different muse about handling life's challenges and finding your true self. (Note: Your true self must be found by the end of the semester.)	Pavilion

8:40 a.m.	**FROM ARISTOTLE TO BERNANKE: FINANCE AND PHILOSOPHY FOR THE SELF-MADE WOMAN** Put your money where your mouth is because smart Alphas finish rich. Philosophy will be your surfboard as you ride the waves of today's economy.	The Acropolis
9:40 am	**ROMANCE LANGUAGES** Be a globe-trotting Alpha in Spanish, French, and Portuguese. A prerequisite for Chinese and Arabic.	Sculpture Garden
10:10 a.m.	**PROTEIN BREAK** Nourish your mind and body with a personalized smoothie. You'll need it!	Health Food Court
10:20 a.m.	**THE ART OF EXCELLENCE** Betas work to live. Alphas live to work. Map your professional goals with a life coach and reach for the stars!	Elizabeth I Lecture Hall
11:30 a.m.	**HONE IT: FOR WRITERS** Whether fact or fiction, when Alphas write, the world reads.	The Fuselage
12:40 p.m.	**LUNCH AND SYMPHONY** Digest lunch and life as you commune with Beethoven, Brahms, and Tchaikovsky.	Pavilion
1:50 p.m.	**GREENER PASTURES** Once you go green, you'll never go back. Learn to keep your footprint small while wearing fabulous shoes.	Biosphere
2:55 p.m.	**SPOTLIGHT TRAINING: POISE IN THE PUBLIC EYE** Achieve poise in the public eye with red carpet, talk show, and political campaign training.	Buddha Building

4:10 p.m	SOCIAL NETWORKING FOR FUTURE MOGULS Go viral and go big. Alphas are what keep the Internet running.	Melinda Gates Computer Lab
5:10 p.m	FIGURE DRAWING It's all in the details. Train your eye, and your hands and spirit will follow.	Sculpture Garden
6:00 p.m	IYENGAR YOGA & MEDITATION Connect with universal oneness—essential to looking out for number one.	Buddha Building Meditation Hall

Allie thought again about going to Shira and telling her she wanted to leave the Academy. But that would mean going home a loser. She would have to face Fletcher and Trina and explain the whole shameful fiasco. Exhaling a rattly sigh, Allie realized she would just have to do what Shira wanted: She would have to find her passion and succeed at it.

Whatever *it* was.

An aPod beeped. Allie looked back down, but it wasn't hers.

"Well, that was fast. It's Darwin!" AJ padded barefoot back from the bathroom. The Jackie O's—everyone but Allie, of course—gathered around her again. Allie swallowed the knot in her throat and pretended to be absorbed in remaking her already-made bed.

"He says he wants to hang. Huge fan, blah blah." AJ scanned the message.

Allie stared at her perfectly tucked-in comforter. She wished she could crawl into bed and never get out. This was agony. How could Darwin move on so quickly?

"Hoo boy," murmured Triple under her breath. She arched a perfectly plucked eyebrow at Allie. "From awkward to awkward-er."

Charlie and Skye were strangely quiet, looking from Allie to AJ and back again.

"How's tonight?" said AJ, reading her message aloud as she typed and pressing SEND before snapping her phone closed with a flourish. "He introduced himself after my performance last night," she announced in her high, breathy voice. "Seems cool for a high school boy. I usually skew older."

Allie's newly navy blue eyes filled with tears for the fourth time that morning. Her gaze was inexorably drawn across the room to Charlie, who was folding a pair of pants with a surgeon's precision, running her finger along a crease again and again. Her friend's jaw pulsed as she stress-chewed the inside of her cheek. Finally, Charlie looked up from the pants, her brown eyes making contact with Allie's. Allie registered a flicker of the same panic over AJ that she herself was feeling. But just as Allie thought that maybe the two friends still had something in common, Charlie looked away, snapping the windows to her soul shut as if Allie was a total stranger.

Hoping the M&M's she'd downed wouldn't make their way back up, Allie bent down to strap on her never-before-used pair of clear gladiator sandals. Back in Santa Ana, her platforms, ballet slippers, boots, and sandals were the envy of all her less-fashionable classmates. But nobody wanted to be in her shoes anymore.

Least of all Allie herself.

11

Sitting in front of forty-four giant computer monitors and listening to the hum of countless hard drives, Charlie should have been excited. A roomful of technology usually made her heart sing and her fingers itch to dive in and explore it. But today, alone in Shira's basement, Charlie's usual enthusiasm had flatlined.

Spotting a stack of *Brazille Hour* Post-it notes, she peeled one off and began impatiently ripping the Shira-emblazoned square into shreds. As the computer rang for the twentieth time, she balled up the paper squares and flicked them at the black monitors. Charlie was trying to reach her old friend Jessupha Rabate. She'd met the tech whiz in Thailand two years ago, when Shira had taken everyone there to set up a manufacturing plant. Jess was the first computer genius Charlie had ever known. He had managed to help Charlie rewire Shira's Palm Pilot as a satellite that could poach

American TV channels. Maybe he could help her rewire Shira's surveillance system, too?

If he ever showed up.

Jessupha Rabate is off-line. Please try again later.

Charlie clicked on the green CALL icon again, drumming her fingers anxiously on the enormous metal desk. As the computer rang, she looked at the ceiling, studying the geometric patterns in its white-tiled surface. A sliver of her brain was occupied with listening for Darwin's footsteps. By the sound of things, he wasn't home.

During each of her seven classes, Charlie's thoughts had ricocheted between anger at Allie and panic over Darwin. Knowing he wasn't home made Charlie's left eye twitch. She pictured him hanging out with AJ. She shivered as she imagined AJ droning on about factory farming in her babyish Paris Hilton–pitched voice while Darwin nodded admiringly. Somehow it felt different—more dangerous— for Darwin to be with AJ. Kind of like AJ was stealing Charlie's soul, or at least her soul mate. And if Darwin spent too much time with the eco-noying AJ, he wouldn't be Charlie's soul mate anymore. He'd be Al Gore.

Beep!

Jessupha Rabate is off-line. Please try again later.

Ugh!

"What am I going to do?" she whined, pounding her forehead with her fist. If she didn't fix the cameras soon, she would miss out on her chance to impress Shira. Even worse, she would practically guarantee a romance between AJ and Darwin.

Charlie took a deep breath and clicked the green CALL button one last time.

"Come on, my little Thai buddy . . . ," she whispered, listening to the computer ring. Jessupha had never let her down before. She thought back to two years ago when they were twelve. Shira and her entourage—including Charlie and her mother—were in Thailand setting up an overseas plant that would employ thousands of operators to take orders for Shira's FEWW (Female Empowerment Workshop Workbooks—thanks to Shira's talk-show promotions, they remained on the *New York Times* bestseller list longer than any other self-help titles). Jessupha's father was hired to run the plant, and he brought Jessupha along to his meetings with Shira as a sort of tween Thai ambassador. Charlie liked Jessupha; he was great with technology and taught her what to order at the local restaurants, explaining that the only way to calm a hot chili overdose was with rice, never water.

But Jessupha more than *liked* Charlie. He luved her. But Charlie *loved* Darwin. Besides, Jessupha may have been a tech whiz, but he was also a scrawny kid with a bad case of early-onset acne and heavy-duty Thai braces on his teeth, with twice as much metal as the American kind. It was a relief for both Darwin and Charlie that Jessupha was un-crushable: If he'd been cuter, Charlie might have fallen for him. Darwin appreciated her talent, but Jessupha furthered it. Their connection was intense but strictly platonic.

"Hi Charlie!" said a deep, Thai-accented voice. Then the video popped up and Charlie had to swallow a gasp. The white-sand beach and teal water behind Jess were just as beautiful as ever, and the calm breezes gently flowing through the leaves of the palm trees made the whole scene look like absolute paradise.

But it was the boy on the beach who was postcard perfect.

"Jessupha?" For a second, Charlie didn't recognize the person staring at her from across the ocean. He had put on at least fifteen pounds of muscle, and above those broad shoulders was creamy Proactiv skin, an Invisalign smile, and the same kind nut-brown eyes as always.

"I go by Jess now," he said in his new baritone voice, looking thrilled to be seeing her again. "It's great to see you, Charlie! I've always wondered why we lost touch."

"I guess I was just busy with school and stuff." She blushed, suddenly self-conscious. If only she'd thought to put on lip gloss and fix her hair before the video chat! But how could she know that her old friend had turned into such a babe? "What have you been up to?" Her voice cracked a little, and she winced inwardly.

"Thai Twitter, of course. I'm developing a lot of applications for that . . . and I'm still hacking phones, just for fun. I turned my iPhone into a hologram projector last week!"

"That's amazing, Jessupha—I mean Jess." A shiver shot up Charlie's spine. She could almost feel Jess's hundred-watt smile melting her brain into gooey marshmallow fluff.

"And what about you, Charlie? Are you"—Jess's voice got even deeper—"still seeing Darwin?"

Charlie glanced behind her at the slice of light under the door at the top of the basement stairs. What if Darwin had come home and was listening in through the door?

"No," she said, clearing her throat, which suddenly felt as if it was stuffed with cotton. "We broke up a little while ago."

Charlie thought she detected a blush creeping up Jess's neck and into his face. "I just broke up with someone, too. A local model. Beautiful but boring. Not everyone can be both gorgeous and brilliant." He smiled meaningfully, sending tingles along Charlie's arms.

Charlie giggled nervously. She leaned out of the camera's view for a second to fan herself with her shirt, desperate to slow down her racing heartbeat. *Computers, Charlie, think about computers.* Sitting upright once more, she changed the subject back to the thing that turned both of them from chic to geek. "Do you think you could help me channel my brilliance a little? We have a serious tech glitch going on here."

"Anything for you, Charlie." He grinned.

Charlie took a deep breath and leaned in closer to the screen, launching into an explanation of how she managed to game her own system.

"Remember how you showed me what I could do to spike a string of HTML and JAVA to kind of trick the phone and override the normal security measures? Well, I did the same thing with our security firewall—" Charlie stopped to wiggle her eyebrows dramatically so Jess would understand she'd sabotaged the security system herself. "And now I can't seem to re-securitize." If Shira was listening, she hoped that what she'd just admitted would go over Shira's technologically inept head.

"Okay, start sending me screenshots of what you're dealing with. I'm sure we can figure it out, easy as cake."

"You mean pie." Charlie giggled. No matter how gorgeous he was on the outside, Jess was still a geek at heart.

Charlie powered up the bank of computers and began the complicated work of unraveling the mess she'd made. Jess helped her troubleshoot the gaps in the code once she was sure she'd correctly rewired the hardware, and after an hour or so and some smart suggestions from Jess, Charlie knew they were on the right track.

"It's getting late. I think I can take it from here," she said. "Let me try some things out and Skype you back tomorrow."

"But, Charlie, I think we're almost done; we just have to look up how to—"

"You don't want to talk again tomorrow?" She tilted her head to one side, daring him to say no.

"Oh! Yeah! Of course!" Jess blush-smiled. "Sure. Try some stuff out and call me."

"Night . . ." Charlie quickly pressed the END button before Jess could see how blotchy her chest had become.

Of course, Charlie wanted to impress Shira and fix the cameras tonight. But Shira had spent fourteen years thinking Charlie was useless—she could wait one or two more days.

After all, Darwin had moved on—he'd moved on *twice*.

Maybe it was time for Charlie to do the same.

12

Flitting around the studio in time with Lady Gaga's "Paparazzi" blasting out of the speakers, Skye was the belle of the ball, the star of the show, and the ringleader of the circus. Her dance party was officially a success. She wore a black leo under a black miniskirt and a coppery Alpha-issue shrug, tying the look together with her resurrected black mesh dance sleeves with charms jingling at her wrists: a horseshoe for luck, a dance shoe for love, a pair of lips for kissing, and a key to the studio that Mimi had given each of the dancers for practicing after hours. Skye had found another use for the key—a party that could get her booted from Alpha Academy faster than the tempo of the final grand jeté in *Swan Lake*—but at least she was keeping it in a safe place!

In a fit of paranoid party prep, Skye had tacked up some bedsheets from the Jackie O house to cover the windows

111

and hide the action inside, but if anyone passed by underneath the clear dance floor, they would get an eyeful of dancers and other Alpha girls shaking their buns to the beat. But the real shock would be seeing the most forbidden and delicious fruit at the Academy: four out of five Brazille Boys. Taz, Syd, Mel, and Dingo had arrived together and turned the room into an insta-party for the boy-starved girls, who buzzed around them like bees in a honeysuckle patch.

Besides Skye, the only Jackie O in attendance was Charlie. Triple would never waste precious sleep time on a party. Not that Skye had invited her. And Allie the Imposter was obviously not welcome.

"One more time! Holo holla!" Skye shouted to Ophelia, who had just figured out how to work Mimi's insta-playback hologram emitter. Five hologram dancers from today's class flickered on in the middle of the dance floor, ball-changing and high-kicking in slo-mo.

"We got this!" said Mel. "Come on, Dingo, let's show them our dance moves!"

Bobbing to the beat, the boys lined up behind the holo-girls, imitating their routine and trying to keep their baggy jeans up while Lady Gaga belted out the chorus.

"And twirl!" shouted Prue. The boys spun around clumsily, reminding Skye of the dancing bears in tutus she'd seen with her mother on a trip to Russia.

"Sharper, Mel, watch that right foot!" added Ophelia, giggling as they gave up and began waving their hands through the flailing arms and legs of the holo-girls.

"You dancers need to eat more!" Mel laughed, sucking in his cheeks. "I can see right through you!"

Taz danced his way over to Skye, put his hands on her shoulders, and whispered in her ear, "Your party's a hit!"

Skye shivered at Taz's touch. He was all confidence in a blazer over an untucked white oxford shirt and khakis. But then Skye looked over at Syd on the other side of the room, every bit as crushable in a pair of distressed black jeans, gray Chucks, and a green hoodie with leather patches on the elbows. He was busy snapping pictures with his aPod and e-mailing them to Skye so they'd never forget the evening. Skye's feelings seemed destined to bounce like a greased pinball from Taz to Syd and back again.

Across the room, Ophelia pushed a button and soon their holo-twins moved in double time. Skye joined them and motioned for Ophelia and Prue to do the same. "Ah-one and two and three and four!"

At the end of the ten-second number, as Skye and the other dancers slid into their closing poses and tried to catch their breath after moving faster than Powerpuff Girls, the rest of the party guests burst out in a rowdy round of applause. Especially Taz and Syd.

Skye smiled at both of them, praying they would each feel like they had her full attention.

"Here's to Skye," said Syd, "for being an awesome dancer and for throwing a great party!"

"To Skye!" a few partiers answered back. Skye curtsy-twirled. Finally, she was the center of attention in a dance studio again. She hadn't felt this appreciated since her days as top banana at BADS.

"Thanks for coming, everyone!" she said, channeling her inner Cat Deeley, the beautiful, poised host of *So You Think You Can Dance*. "And thanks to Charlie for turning off the cameras! We wouldn't be here without her!"

Charlie wave-shrugged as another smattering of applause rippled through the room. "No biggie," she said.

"Okay," Skye said, "let's do the routine again in triple time!" She was eating up the attention like pizza bagels after a week of Atkins.

"Mmkay, lemme just figure out which button . . ." Ophelia studied Mimi's remote control as Lady Gaga faded into a Kanye West track.

But before the holo-girls were cued up again, the elevator doors slid open, revealing AJ in a shaggy faux-fur jacket, her guitar slung over one arm and Darwin on the other.

"Hey," she drawled, her voice languid and scratchy like her vocal cords needed a break. "Cool space." She walked over and joined Skye in the center of the room, took off her jacket, and proceeded to sit on it cross-legged, as if the dance studio were a campfire jamboree. Seemingly oblivious to the Kanye blasting from the speakers and Skye's attempts to keep dancing, AJ took a guitar pick out of her pocket and started playing her usual eco-folk.

"AJ, should we maybe do that later? This is a dance par—," Skye started.

"But I wrote you guys a new song." AJ looked up at Skye and smiled reassuringly, as if now that she had arrived, the party was officially awesome.

Skye glared down at AJ's pale, mousy face framed by black tendrils and wondered for the first time if Imposter Allie wasn't a slightly better alternative to the real thing. Imposter Allie would never barge into a party and take over—it wasn't her style.

AJ traced a circle in the air with one tiny, unmanicured finger, and before Skye could think of a way to regain control of the room, everyone gathered around like it was time for show-and-tell and AJ was the kindergarten teacher.

"Turn down the music!" someone yelled. "We can't hear AJ!"

Ophelia turned off the Kanye, shrugging at Skye.

Skye looked at Charlie, who was staring at Darwin like she'd just eaten a bad piece of sushi.

There's a little group of chicks I know
They call themselves the Jackie O's
They put their friends ahead of the Brazille bros
(Except for one girl, a fake, a faux—)
But the truth won out and the lies exposed
And now the Jackie O's are friends, not foes,
Because they have talent that naturally shows.

As AJ sang, Skye's turquoise eyes met Charlie's toffee-brown ones and silently beamed a message: *SOS!*

It wasn't just that AJ was stealing Skye's thunder—though that didn't help. It was that the song seemed cheap. AJ had been a Jackie O for exactly *one* day—she hardly even *knew* them.

Charlie crossed her eyes and sucked in her cheeks, silently stabbing an imaginary knife repeatedly into her own chest.

Skye giggled. But all around her, Skye's wild party had turned into a mellow folk-fest. The songstress was sucking up the attention in the room faster than a Dirt Devil. Skye bit her lower lip in fury. Did the girl have a MUTE button?

Nope.

"Shout out a word and I'll turn it into song lyrics," she commanded as she strummed her guitar. Her grass-green eyes circled the room, daring anyone to say no.

"Butt crack!" shouted Taz. Was it his way of derailing AJ

and putting the focus back on Skye? Or was he just goofing around?

"But crack the surface and take a look," sang AJ. *"You can't cover up an open book. . . ."*

"Wannabe!" Syd yelled, winking at Skye.

Skye shivered pleasantly; his intention was clear. Her party may have gotten the kiss of death from AJ, but if she was lucky, she might be kissing one of the brothers before the night was over.

"People will be who they wanna be," AJ warbled. *"So nurture your spirit organically. . . ."*

People started shouting out words left and right. Apparently, cheesy songwriting made a good party trick. Skye glowered at the enthusiastic crowd. She had a few choice words of her own for this eco-maniac.

"One-trick pony!" she shouted.

But of course AJ spun Skye's words into green gold.

"Thought you were a one-trick pony," the beastly brunette sang, *"but you pranced in and became my one and only!"*

Skye looked around helplessly as everyone in the room swayed to the rhythm of AJ's music. *What happened to my big night?* Skye's lungs were starting to tighten. She walked toward the corner of the room and lifted the edge of one of the sheets she'd painstakingly tacked up to crack the window and get a whiff of jasmine-scented air.

Just when Skye was rebounding from all of Mimi's abuse,

just when she'd started to feel like there was something at the Academy that she might be the best at, someone had to show her up. She couldn't win! Everywhere she turned, some girl was there to outdo her. Triple out-danced her in class, and now AJ was out-partying her at her big event. Skye pulled her heel against her butt and felt the sweet burn of her quad stretching out. At least she still had two boys to choose from, she reminded herself.

She closed the window and began to move in Syd's direction, until she noticed him rocking back and forth on his heels and clapping, singing along with AJ like he was her biggest fan. Skye pursed her lips and whipped around on her heels. She didn't want to look at Syd for one more second.

Decision made: Syd is out!

Her face hot with anger and humiliation, Skye stood on her tiptoes and searched out Taz. *I knew it all along,* she thought, clinging to the one positive thing about tonight. *Taz's obvious-leh meant for me.*

But when her eyes finally landed on Taz, he was kneeling in the middle of the circle. He had taken a pair of decorative toe shoes off the wall and was using them as castanets, banging them together in time with AJ's freaky folk song. Skye could see sweat glistening along his hairline, proving just how into AJ's music he was. He was totally hooked by AJ, too! *Has everyone gone bananas?!*

Both boys had tossed her out quicker than a used-up wad

of gum. If everyone weren't singing along with AJ, Skye was certain they would hear the *splat* of her heart bouncing out of her rib cage and onto the dance floor.

"Your toxic ways pollute my ozone," sang the green guitarist as Skye seethed with toxic green envy. *"You're headed from yes right into my no-zone!"*

Stalking around the edge of the jam session like a caged leopard, Skye did the only thing she could. A tight smile played on Skye's lips as she began to plot her revenge.

HAD No. 7: Tear AJ a new ozone-size hole!

13

Charlie stared helplessly at her right elbow. She could almost feel the heat from Darwin's arm two inches away from hers. Her eyes followed his sleeve up to where it attached to his body and traced the profile of his face with her eyes, just like she used to do when they were a couple. She could scream out his name right now and he wouldn't even notice. He was too busy swaying back and forth to the sounds of AJ's pretentious crooning, staring at the songstress with the kind of adoration and pride that used to be reserved for Charlie.

Sighing, she spotted Taz standing on the other side of the pulsating circle of revelers with AJ at its center. He danced along with the music, clapping a set of ballet slippers together in time with the song. Syd, who was usually so remote and withdrawn and always hated crowds, seemed to have gotten over his agoraphobic tendencies. He clapped in time with AJ's song, too, nodding at the skin-deep lyrics, cheesy rhymes about oil slicks and dirty tricks. Even Melbourne and Dingo had stopped clowning around and checking out girls to rock out with AJ.

It was official: Every one of the Brazille brothers was caught in AJ's eco-net.

Charlie felt the heat rise in her cheeks. The dance studio was suddenly more suffocating than a too-tight turtleneck. She used to be the girl the Brazille brothers all adored—she was the sister, the girlfriend. The one they all secretly wanted to date. One Mother's Day three years ago, Dingo had asked her if she would be his mum instead of Shira. If that wasn't love and adoration, Charlie didn't know what was. But her lifetime spent with the Brazille Boys clearly meant nothing to them now. Charlie was just another uniformed Alpha girl, and AJ's star power had eclipsed even the shiniest of them. Next to her, a normal Alpha was practically a beta.

AJ may have been green, but Charlie was greener. Her envy was off the charts, so thick she was choking on it.

Allie A may have been a liar and a fraud, but at least she had made an effort to be a good friend, to really get to know the Jackie O's, especially Charlie. She was a fraud, and yet she was so much *realer* than AJ would ever be. *But why did she have to lie?* Even though she was in a room packed with people, Charlie felt totally alone.

Bee had always told her that sometimes the only cure for

loneliness was being alone. *It's worth a try*, Charlie thought. If she spent much longer at this party, she might need professional help to fully recover.

Just as she was preparing to bolt for a long walk and a hot bath, her aPod beeped.

SHIRA: THE CAMERAS ARE STILL OFF—I NEED TO KNOW WHO'S SNEAKING AROUND AFTER LIGHTS-OUT. ANY NAMES FOR ME YET?

Ugh! Couldn't Shira ever give it a rest?

Charlie: No names yet . . .

When Charlie looked up from her phone, the group had devolved into an impromptu jam session. Everyone but Skye was banging on something or clapping their hands, and Taz and Dingo had taken over on AJ's guitar. With the jam session raging, nobody would even notice she was gone.

She walked across the bouncy dance floor, staring at her gladiator sandals and counting the seconds until she was under a canopy of trees with nobody to keep her company but some cooing doves and a few chirping crickets. That was the kind of jam session she needed right now.

"Hey," AJ murmured, startling Charlie by insinuating

her petite frame between Charlie's hand and the elevator button. "Leaving already?"

"Yeah," Charlie answered, taking a cautious step to the side and reaching around AJ's tiny waist to press the down arrow. Couldn't AJ get in someone else's face for a while? "I'm surprised you noticed."

AJ looked up at her and leaned in close enough for Charlie to smell her patchouli essential oil perfume. *Gag!* Charlie made a mental note to mouth-breathe exclusively when AJ was within close range of her nostrils.

"Of course I noticed! You're my roommate. I pay attention to my roommates." A smile flickered across her rosebud lips and she picked some invisible lint off Charlie's sleeve. "Are you going to Shira's office?"

Huh? What did this girl *want*? Charlie's heart began to race. "Why would you ask that?"

"Oh, Shira mentioned the two of you were old friends." AJ's cloudy green eyes stared past Charlie and focused on Darwin, who was now strumming her guitar.

"*Friends* is not the word for what we are," sighed Charlie. *Not that it should matter to* you. She stared at the indicator light above the elevator. What was taking so long?

"Well, if you're looking for someone to kick out, pick that girl by the window." AJ pointed to a willowy Mary-Kate Olsen look-alike named Helene, a drama-tracked Alpha who was writing a dystopian play about the economy called *Blair Waldorf Works at Burger King Now.* "She's been sneaking cigarettes all night. Did you know they fill the air with many of the same poisons found in the air around toxic waste dumps? So disgusting. Not to mention secondhand smoke kills over fifty thousand people every year. Smoking is just like committing murder, if you think about it. Just being around it tears my vocal cords to ribbons."

"What?" Charlie was shocked. Why was AJ telling her to get someone kicked out? The whole studio began to spin as Charlie's panic intensified. "What did you say?"

"Cigarettes fill the air with the same toxins as—"

"No." Charlie spoke warily. "I *know* about cigarettes being bad. The part about me kicking someone out is what I didn't understand." Only the Jackie O's knew that Charlie was being forced to spy for Shira. Which one of them told AJ? And who would AJ tell? Had she already written a song about it?

"I know you're spying. I heard you guys talking about it at the Jackie O house."

"When? You just got here!" Charlie's danger sensors had gone from code orange to code red as she racked her brain trying to remember when the Jackie O's had brought up her secret.

"I'm not an idiot, Charlie. I won't tell anyone. Of course, if she sticks around much longer"—AJ stuck out her pale, pointy chin to indicate Helene, who was unwrapping a piece of gum and walking back over to join the jam session—"I might *accidentally* leak the information."

The only smoke in the studio now was coming straight out of Charlie's ears.

"Thanks for the heads-up." Charlie hate-smiled, clenching her fists to try to keep them from shaking with rage. "Now if you'll excuse me, I'm leaving."

"Bye!" AJ yelled cheerfully, grabbing a handful of the long silver necklaces she wore draped around her neck and shaking it like a dog toy. Her eco-ditz persona was firmly reattached, but now Charlie knew the manipulative schemer lurking beneath AJ's flaky exterior.

"See you," Charlie hissed as the elevator doors dinged shut. She wished it could be good-bye forever. AJ might have been used to getting whatever she wanted in her life as a rock star, but Alpha Island was Charlie's arena. She resolved to begin planning her next tactical maneuver in the war to stay on the island.

Operation Destroy AJ was officially under way.

14

With two pillows beneath her head, one under her knees, and one to clutch in her arms like a feather-filled, squishy version of Darwin, Allie should have been asleep long ago. She had counted everything she could think of: sheep, birds, stars, boys she'd crushed on, shoes she'd bought at the Santa Ana mall, states she'd visited, rom-coms she'd seen more than once—but sleep still eluded her. She listened to Triple's rhythmic breathing and thought about throwing something at her. A pissed-off Triple might be more fun than hours of lonely insomnia.

Allie and Triple had the room all to themselves, not that they had much to say to each other. The rest of the Jackie O's were at Skye's party, but Skye hated Triple and now she hated Allie even more. Even if she had been invited, Allie wouldn't have gone. Everyone there was still mad at her, and she needed to stay horizontal after an exhausting day of following her new schedule, where one class was more disastrous than the next.

Class

BREAKFAST AND MOTIVATIONAL LECTURE	Finally, no wheat-meat! But nine strips of bacon + anxiety = ick.
FROM ARISTOTLE TO BERNANKE: FINANCE AND PHILOSOPHY FOR THE SELF-MADE WOMAN	News flash: Plato entirely unrelated to Play-Doh.
ROMANCE LANGUAGES	Still ill from breakfast, Allie accidentally claims *en français* that her B-cups are on fire. ("I meant heart! I have a warm heart!")
PROTEIN BREAK	At the nutritional vending machine, Allie finds a spitball in her hair. *Ew!*
THE ART OF EXCELLENCE	Write a five-year plan? Allie can't even get through the next five hours!
HONE IT: FOR WRITERS	Darwin calls Allie's poem about forgiveness a bad AJ knockoff. Tears, followed by hyperventilating.
LUNCH AND SYMPHONY	Allie tries to zone out and absorb a Brahms concerto, but Darwin and AJ sit directly in front of her and whisper the whole time. She leaves in tears.
GREENER PASTURES	Today's class was on urban composting. Turned out this meant working with a bucket of worms. Allie faints, is sent to the school nurse.

SPOTLIGHT TRAINING: POISE IN THE PUBLIC EYE	Asked to recite something she remembers well, Allie does a scene from *Ten Things I Hate About You*. Skye follows up with an original work: *Ten Things I Hate About Fake Roommates*.
SOCIAL NETWORKING FOR FUTURE MOGULS	Opening her MySpace account for the first time in weeks, she sees it's been hacked. Her picture has been replaced by a video of her crying onstage with AJ.
FIGURE DRAWING	Skipped it. Too busy sobbing.
IYENGAR YOGA & MEDITATION	Allie pulls a muscle during crow pose, squeals like a stuck pig.

Allie tried again to tune out the sound of Triple's perfectly timed breathing. She stared at the ceiling and wished for sleep to put her out of today's misery, but she was too keyed up. Then she heard the glass door slide open downstairs. Allie shut her eyes tightly, cringing like a soldier in a foxhole, hoping whoever came in wouldn't hurl any emotional grenades her way.

She heard the rustling of Charlie's covers in the bed next to hers and hesitantly lifted one eyelid, not sure if she should be relieved or terrified. Allie missed Charlie so much, but she knew her lies hurt Charlie worst of all. It seemed logical to assume Charlie would retaliate somehow. Through one slitted eye, she watched her ex-friend kick off her shoes and crawl into bed without bothering to brush her teeth, wash her face, or even change her clothes.

Probably just doesn't want Thalia to catch her.

On the other hand, everyone knew Thalia slept like the dead.

Ohmuhgud, is she crying?

Pretending to toss in her sleep, Allie turned to face Charlie's bed and get a better look. Her former bestie's shoulders were shaking as silent tears streamed down her cheeks. Allie's throat immediately tightened, filling with salty sympathy tears. She had to try to comfort Charlie somehow, even if her former friend hated her right now. Allie pushed a hand through her brittle dyed-black hair and racked her brain for a surefire way to cheer anyone up. An instant later, it came to her: *rom-coms!*

"Hey Charlie," she whispered.

Charlie put both hands over her eyes and flipped onto her back. "What?" she whisper-spat flatly.

"Remember what happens at the end of *The Ugly Truth?*"

Charlie took one hand away and stared at Allie like she was a recently escaped mental patient.

"Maybe you missed it. It came out last year and starred Katherine Heigl? Anyway, just, if you haven't found a happy ending yet, it means it's not the end." Allie smiled in a way she hoped looked reassuring, wishing she could take her own advice once in a while.

Charlie furrowed her eyebrows and glared at Allie for a beat before flipping over and turning her back on her.

Before Allie could decide what to do next, she heard the sliding glass door open again. Skye teetered up the stairs in high-heeled booties and headed to the bathroom, slamming the door behind her. Allie could hear Skye's toiletries being tossed around, followed by the sounds of an angry face being washed, exfoliated, and moisturized.

"Wha's going on?" Triple lifted her eye mask to peer out from under swollen, sleep-addled lids.

Skye stomped out of the bathroom, now clad in a shorty nightgown and a *don't mess with me* expression aimed squarely at Triple.

"Oh, great—everyone's up!" Skye's voice dripped with sarcasm as she collapsed onto a corner of Charlie's bed. "You missed a great party, Trip. Until our lovely roomie AJ showed up."

Skye sighed dramatically.

Charlie sat up in bed next to Skye, her eyes swollen not from sleep but from her recent pity party. "She tried to blackmail me tonight. She said she knew I was Shira's spy and that if I didn't get a girl kicked out for smoking that she would tell the whole school."

"Ohmuhgud," Triple moaned, pulling her mask down

and settling back into bed. "Will the drama never end? Let's think about it quietly and discuss in the morning."

Skye stared at Charlie, her mouth a perfect O of shock and dismay. Allie took a deep breath and decided to try to fill the silence and comfort Charlie.

"She's toxic. What a waste." Allie murmured her semi-lame pun in a quiet voice, seeing a chance to earn back some of her friend status now that AJ was on everyone's hit list.

Charlie and Skye looked at her and giggled, and Allie felt her ears go hot with relief. At last, the Jackie O ice might be thawing. *Maybe they'll forget how much they hate me!*

"Quiet!" Triple ordered. "Some of us need our sleep! Some of us actually care about *school*, mmmkay?"

"Speaking of toxic," Skye giggled, jabbing a thumb in Triple's direction.

"That's it!" Triple threw her mask to the floor, leapt out of bed, and sashayed over to Skye like Heidi Klum about to take down a *Project Runway* contestant. She grabbed Skye's mesh dance sleeves and pulled them off Skye's arms, ignoring Skye's protesting squeals.

"Triple, these have sentimental value!" Skye thrashed, but Triple had three inches on her and pinned her down.

"This is for your own good!" Triple wrapped the sleeves around Skye's mouth and tied a knot in them before she flounced back to bed in a mock-huff.

"Ooof!" Skye yanked her sleeves down around her neck, rolling her eyes semi-affectionately.

Triple sat back in her bed and turned to Allie, looking genuinely puzzled. "Are your eyes *blue*? Were they always blue?"

"Well," stalled Allie. The last thing she wanted was to spoil this bonding session by reminding everyone about her deception. "Yeah, they've always been blue."

On the other side of her bed, Charlie twirled a brown lock of hair around her fingers the way she did when she was lost in thought. "We need to figure out how to force AJ out."

Skye nodded aggressively in agreement, looking up at the glass-domed ceiling as if the stars could provide some guidance.

"But how?" Allie wondered. To get kicked out of Alpha Academy, Shira had to want you gone.

"Put Krazy Glue on her guitar strings?" Skye tried. Charlie and Allie snort-chuckled.

"Or," Allie chimed in, emboldened by being treated like part of the group again, "we could take pictures of me dressed up as her eating burgers, wearing fur, and, like, clubbing penguins, and we could post them on MySpace!"

This time, nobody laughed. *Too soon?* Allie stared at AJ's unmade bed and wrinkled her nose. AJ's shiny white coverlet was crumpled on the floor, and her tangled sheets were covered in glittery necklaces, dirty laundry, schoolbooks, and makeup. For such an eco-nut, AJ really didn't take very good care of her personal environment.

Triple sleep-sighed from her bed on the far side of the room, having checked out on ditching AJ in favor of catching z's.

Charlie's aPod buzzed with a new text. "How does she know I'm awake?" she whine-groaned, collapsing back into bed.

"Who?" Skye asked.

"Shira! Ever since the cameras went down, she's been begging me for names. Did you guys notice that Shira called twelve names for elimination, but only eleven girls left the Pavilion? I fed her a fake name—Ivy Lambert. I guess she still hasn't found out, because now she wants more!" Charlie groan-sighed, throwing her hands up hopelessly.

"Poor Ivy. She was out of her league." Skye giggle-smirked, wiping away an imaginary tear.

"I always thought she had kind of a poisonous personality, though," Allie said, and the three Jackie O's giggled. It felt so good to be part of the crew again! Allie looked around at her house-mates, praying things would stay like this and Imposter Allie would finally be dead and gone. Maybe this was the fresh start Thalia was talking about—now that she was free to be herself, perhaps Allie A would be a lot more fun than Allie J could ever be.

"Wait," Skye whisper-screamed, leaping up from Charlie's bed. "That's it!"

"What?" said Allie.

"Charlie can turn AJ in for something." Skye stood up and began to twirl-pace, rubbing her palms together the way movie villains did when they hatched a plan. She was Cruella De Vil and Lord Voldemort rolled into one. "I can't believe we didn't think of this sooner. . . ." Skye trailed off, lost in thought.

"Great idea," said Charlie, already typing a message to Shira on her phone. But then she stopped. "What should I say?"

Allie smiled, suddenly knowing exactly what it should be. A perfect synchronicity had visited the Jackie O's, and soon everything would go back to the way it was. "Tell the truth: Say she's been hanging around Darwin!" If it worked, Allie thought, the plan would lead to her getting her friends back. And if she was lucky, maybe even more.

"Okay, here goes," Charlie mumbled, typing fast and furious before she had time to overthink and delete. "Aaaand—message sent!" The three of them waited, blinking at one another and listening to Triple sawing logs.

Ten agonizing seconds later, Charlie's aPod beeped.

"Well?" whispered Skye.

SHIRA: DARWIN IS A VERY GOOD CATCH.
GIRLS ARE GOING TO WANT TO HANG
AROUND HIM. YOU'D BETTER GET USED TO
IT. NOW GET ME SOME REAL NAMES!

Skye collapsed on the floor, curling up like an unwatered houseplant.

As the three girls whisper-groaned in unison, the door downstairs slid open again. AJ's patchouli essential oil found Allie's nostrils, and in a moment AJ herself appeared at the top of the stairs, wrapped in a mangy faux-fur coat that looked like she'd rescued it from a Dumpster.

"Hey ladies," AJ drawled. "Fun night, right?"

Allie's eyes stung as her new roommate came closer. In the semi-dark room, she could make out a cinnamon-scented toothpick dangling from AJ's ChapSticked mouth.

"Yeah. Super-fun," said Skye flatly.

"Hey," Allie whispered, swallowing a scream of frustration. She glanced over at the clock—1:03! Allie didn't want to imagine AJ locking lips with Darwin for hours on end, but her mind couldn't go anywhere else.

"Let's strategize in the bathroom," Skye whispered to Charlie, turning her back on AJ and Allie. "*Alone.*"

Charlie shot an unsmiling look at Allie before rolling out of bed and padding after Skye. Soon, Allie heard the sound of the bathroom door locking followed by muffled giggles. On her own again, Allie pulled her comforter up to her neck and wished again for sleep to put her out of her misery for a few hours.

AJ changed into a pair of pearl-pink pajamas and laid down on Renee's bed, flashing Allie a smug smile. "No wonder you wanted to be me. My life rocks."

For the first time that night, Allie wished she was still masquerading as the Queen of Green. She was trying to be herself, to prove that the real Allie was somebody, too, but the real Allie didn't have much to offer. She had no talent, no special *thing* that was hers. Her friends were having private bathroom conferences without her, and AJ and Darwin were moving faster than the personal Alpha planes that waited to fly boring Allie back home if she failed here.

Not only did Allie have no friends and no talent, she had no hope.

15

Skye stared at herself in the bathroom mirror, adjusting the dial on the wall from "Flattering" to "Pore Examination" light. *Yikes!* Rubbing her eyes, she forced herself to stare hard at the girl reflected back at her under blinding full-spectrum lighting meant only to help catch errant eyebrow hairs and blackheads, not for soul-searching in the middle of the night. Two words came to mind, both starting with *H* and both the opposite of "hot": *haggard, hideous*. She turned the dial back to "Flattering," but even in the pinkish glow, she looked more crumpled than a leg warmer without a leg. She was tired, of course—it had been a crazy day and a busy night and it was now past her internal clock's normal bedtime—but her spirit, the light in her eyes that showed the world Skye Hamilton was fun and fabulous, looked dulled and dim. Her once-sparkly Tiffany-box blue eyes were as faded as stonewashed jeans,

137

her makeup smeared around them in bruisey, vaguely frightening patches.

Skye had spent her whole life at the top of the food chain, always ranked first in dance class, always among the most popular girls in school. Ever since she could remember, boys loved her and girls wanted to be her. But now that Triple had officially been crowned queen bun-head and AJ had pulled an Edward Cullen and sucked all the joy from her party, Skye was in free fall. She should have been the star tonight, and the fact that she couldn't yank her party out of AJ's guitar-playing hands proved that she was losing her Skye-ness—the magical It factor that had always landed her on top.

First, Triple had beaten her in the dance studio, and now AJ had bested her at hosting parties. The boys loved her lyrics and grooved to her beats, rocking out like they were extras in an Allie J music video. So what was Skye good for?

"Still awake?" As if she had been summoned by Skye's thoughts, AJ suddenly appeared in Skye's flattering mirror light. Skye jumped, knocking an open bottle of foundation into the sink.

Great. Now she wouldn't even be able to hide her under-eye bags tomorrow. Yet another thing AJ took without asking.

"Sorry. You can use my makeup if you want. It's bareMinerals. Totally natural, chemical free, and good for the—" AJ's monotonous earth-mama singsong had quickly gone from annoying to unbearable, and Skye couldn't take another syllable.

"First," Skye screech-blurted, "I'm allergic to talc, so bareMinerals gives me hives. And second, in case you didn't notice, my skin has yellow undertones and yours has blue. So obvious-leh we can't share foundation!" Twisting the cap back on her Lancôme bottle as tightly as possible, she wished her fingers were wrapped around AJ's neck instead.

"Oh well," AJ said brightly, taking a wooden toothbrush out of a small wooden case. "Great party tonight. Everyone's still texting about my little impromptu show."

As Skye began squeezing toothpaste onto her electric toothbrush, her hands trembled with rage. *Impromptu! Right.*

"How awesome for you," she finally managed to say over the hum of her Sonicare. *Remain calm,* she told herself. If AJ saw how jealous Skye was, then the party-terrorist had already won. "You've had a big first week here."

"Yeah, I guess. I just do what I do, you know? For some reason, people seem to love it." AJ shrugged, spitting a blob of toothpaste into the sink.

"That's how life was for me once, back home," Skye caught herself admitting.

"Was it?" AJ said, flashing Skye a pity-smile and heading to the eucalyptus-scented Vichy shower. From behind the frosted glass, she added: "Never woulda guessed."

Skye stared at her reflection again, taking a deep sniff of calming eucalyptus and clamping her mouth shut so she wouldn't blurt out something she would later regret. Everyone was obsessing about AJ, eating up her Pop-Tart personality without tasting the bitter saccharine that lay beneath. Skye couldn't compete with AJ's fame, but she couldn't let the green meanie steamroll her spirit.

Desperate for a sign, she scanned the touch-screen controls on the side of the mirror until she found the personal affirmation button, marked with a bubbly set of quotation marks. The mirror beeped, and a moment later produced a glowing neon-pink sentence that slid along the glass and stopped just under Skye's chin.

Personal affirmation for SKYE HAMILTON:
Love looks through a telescope. Envy, through a microscope.

Huh?
Skye spit a blob of toothpaste into the bowl and undertook a final mirror-nalysis as she tried to figure out what the mirror wanted her to do. Blond hair—check. Big green eyes—check. But the eyes needed their magic back. Her mouth was twisted in an unattractive sneer, and her sinewy body was stooped with the weight of the world—AJ's world—on her shoulders. How would she get her mojo back? Where would she find her telescope?

And then it came to her. What do you do when someone steals your thunder? Steal it back, of course. Show her up. Skye had to throw an even bigger party—one so fabulous that there was no way AJ could find a way to ruin it. It had to be someplace that didn't work well for guitar playing, someplace where Skye could divide and conquer the crowd if she needed to. She thought back to some of her best parties back home, remembering golf-cart racing at the country club, dance parties in abandoned swimming pools, subway-car takeovers—that was it!

Deep in thought, Skye high-kicked her leg and pressed her calf against her forehead, enjoying the tingle of exertion that traveled from her hip to her ankle. Lowering her leg to the floor, she blew her mirror image an air kiss. She was a genius! Her next party would be the talk of the school for months. Her new plan firmly fixed in her mind, Skye smiled at the mirror now—not just with her mouth but with her eyes. She grabbed her aPod from the bathroom counter and texted Taz with her idea.

Her phone beeped three seconds later.

Taz: PARTY TRAIN!!!

Would Syd's response be even more enthusiastic? Only one way to find out! Skye sent him the same message she'd sent Taz:

Skye: Friday at midnight, let's have an even bigger bash. Only this time, we'll take the party on the road, or at least bubble-train tracks—gotta carpe diem while the cameras are down! Skye's the limit!

Skye waited impatiently for Syd's response. It took ten times longer than Taz's to arrive, and when it did, her chugging heart slammed to a stop.

Syd: Shouldn't you be using your energy to dance? And what if you get caught? I thought you were more than just a party girl.

Staring at her reflection in the mirror, her blond waves a little bit frizzy from AJ's steamy shower, Skye felt a deep blush of shame stain her skin. How embarrassing to come *this close* to falling for the wrong guy! She was mortified not to have noticed it sooner: Sydney was a total wuss.

16

Charlie examined her face in the shiny rectangular reflection of the laptop screen: big brown eyes (her best feature, she'd always thought); adequate lips (semi-rosebud, neither full nor thin, with a light coat of tinted ChapStick, since lipstick made her feel overdone); long, chestnut-brown, good-hair-day hair (yes!). Leaning in closer to the laptop, Charlie pinched her cheeks for color. Then she wiped her sweaty hands on her new Alpha uniform, a belted shirtdress in shimmery copper that had recently been introduced to their wardrobe.

Over the years, Darwin had seen her at her ugliest. He'd been with her when she got food poisoning in Barcelona, renaming the city "Barf-celona"; when she contracted an unfortunate case of forehead zits just before Darwin's thirteenth birthday party (a hair spray allergy, she'd lied); and when an African mantis had bitten her eyelid, making her look like a newborn gerbil. After a boy saw you like that, being pretty didn't seem as important.

Thinking about *her* Darwin and the Darwin she witnessed last night, the one who hung on AJ's every obnoxious word, made Charlie want to find a hammer and smash a few of the monitor screens. How could he not see how manipulative AJ was? Or worse: What if he saw it and *liked* it? It was too much to contemplate. Charlie clicked on the green Skype icon and resolved to put Darwin out of her mind for now and focus on Jess.

Jess picked up her call after just one ring. His smile was as white as the sand of the beach behind him. He looked as if he smelled like salt and cocoa butter.

"Hi Charlie." Jess smiled. Charlie wished there was something more interesting behind her than boxes of computer equipment. "So . . . did you fix the cameras yet?"

Charlie had, in fact, figured it out. She just had to connect a circuit to the breaker and the security system would be up and running. But she wasn't ready to do that just yet. If she fixed the cameras entirely, what excuse would she have to Skype with Jess?

"I think I'm almost there," she lied, testing out a few eyelash bats. She'd read somewhere that this was a sure-fire attractor of the opposite sex, and that it worked for ostriches, llamas, and other not-so-hot animals. And while Charlie didn't feel as beautiful as some of the Alphas, she was certainly a lot cuter than a llama. "Thanks to you, that is." Charlie pretended to fiddle with a motherboard on an open desktop in front of her.

"Me? It was all you," Jess said. He was still modest to a fault. "I just pulled the donkey."

"Pulled the donkey?" Charlie laughed and blushed a deeper shade of pink, cocking her head to one side. Was Jess likening her to a farm animal or just botching an expression?

"No donkey? Bad translation. Um . . . hang on." Jess smiled sheepishly and typed something into his iPhone. "Okay . . . I just greased the wheels. You steered the bus."

"Well, it was a joint effort." Charlie grinned. "Kinda like the time we rigged Mel's phone to play 'My Humps' on repeat every time he turned it on." Charlie giggled at the memory. Jess had been horrified when she'd suggested it, but he loved figuring out how to pull the prank.

Jess laughed, the corners of his eyes curling up affectionately. "So funny! Until he threw it in the ocean. After that, I felt bad. Did he ever find out who did it?"

"Yeah. I'm still waiting for him to get back at me." Charlie smiled. "And I'm pretty sure he's still mad at you."

"There's nobody here like you, Charlie. Brains and beauty," Jess continued. "Every boy you know has a crush on you, I'm sure."

That might have been true once, Charlie conceded.

Back when she was the planet around which the Brazille Boys orbited. Back when there weren't dozens of shiny, smiling Alphas to distract each one of them.

Jess's iPhone trilled. "Gotta take this, Charlie. Can you hold on? It's my dad."

"Sure," she said, and Jess jumped out of his chair and began to pace the beach.

Charlie sighed, thinking about the insurmountable distance between them. Absence made the heart grow fonder, though, didn't it? At least that was how it worked for Charlie's mom and dad. Before her dad died, he had been a member of the Royal Navy, monitoring peace-keeping operations in Bosnia. Bee and Charles (Charlie was named for her dad) only saw each other a few days a month, when Charles was off duty. Charlie still had stacks of letters they sent to each other, and part of her always thought she'd have a similar long-distance romance. But the way Bee coped with Charles being so far away was gab-bing with her two closest friends, Hildy and Mare. In talk-ing about Charles with her two best girlfriends, Bee kept him near her heart.

Charlie flipped open the locket on her cameo bracelet, the one that held her father's picture inside. He stared back at her, his Royal Navy hat perched just so, his kind eyes reminding her that life was shorter than high school often led you to believe. It flew by in a minute. Charlie flipped open the other cameo to the place Darwin's picture used to be, but Shira had taken it away from her when she'd accepted her into Alpha Academy.

Looking at that blank oval where Darwin's face once belonged, Charlie had a sudden, fierce pang of missing Allie. Allie was the one person on this island who would appreciate the tragic romance of her flirtation with Jess. She would eat up Charlie's Skype hype about how cute Jess had become. Charlie clicked the cameo closed with a sigh—she couldn't talk to Allie. They just weren't friends anymore. Allie had lied, and their friendship was built under false pretenses. Then again, Charlie had lied once, too—to get into Shira's school.

Charlie sat back with a thud. The more she thought about it, the more obvious it became: She and Allie had both sold their souls to get into Alpha Academy. Like Jess said, they had given up so much for the chance to shine for Shira. And at least Allie didn't hurt anyone she loved to go here! Charlie had wanted admission badly enough to get her mom fired and break her boyfriend's heart. All Allie had done was dye her hair and draw a mole on her upper lip. It wasn't so awful, now that Charlie thought about it. It was nothing that Charlie wouldn't have done herself if she'd been in Allie's shoes.

Charlie's heart began to beat faster than the wings of the mechanical butterflies she'd built to teach herself circuitry.

She had to get out of here ASAP. She had to make things right with Allie.

"Jess!" she called, waving at the figure pacing the beach to sit down at his laptop again. When he saw her waving, he said good-bye to his dad on the phone and sat back down.

"Sorry about that." He smiled.

Even though Jess was adorable, Charlie didn't have any time to waste.

"Can I Skype you tomorrow? There's somewhere I have to be," she said. She buckled her gladiator sandals around her ankles as she talked, her mind already back at Jackie O with Allie.

"Of course," Jess said, running his hand through his thick black hair. "Call me every day!"

Charlie felt a tingle run down her spine. If things went the way she hoped, maybe tomorrow she would tell Jess all about her new friend, Allie—the girl who did the gutsiest thing to get into Alpha Academy. Well, the second gutsiest.

17

Allie wondered if anyone had ever been driven insane by tropical birds before. She prodded at her makeshift earplugs, two balled-up strips of toilet paper cribbed from the Jackie O bathroom, and wished they actually worked to block out the squawking macaw that had planted itself outside Jackie O.

"Aren't you supposed to sleep at night?" Allie yelled. She remembered that much from biology class—birds were diurnal, not nocturnal like bats.

But the macaw had clearly not taken seventh-grade bio with mustachioed Mrs. Wilson, because it squawked back a shrill reply that sounded like, "Nosiree!"

Allie shivered in the night air, pulling her blanket around her shoulders. If she was going to spend another night on the chaise longue, at least this time she'd brought essentials. She had her pillow and blanket and all the books from her gazillion-class schedule to keep her company. And she had her pride! She couldn't bear the thought of another night spent "sleeping" (more like staring at the floating numerals of the digital clock in abject misery, since she wasn't getting any actual sleep) amid a group of girls who all hated her. She'd take the chaise longue any day over that.

Allie stared down at the books and assignments piled around her. She couldn't focus on any of them. None of her classes were *her*; nothing stuck out as a subject she could be passionate about. And the dyed-black hair that was taking forever to grow out, well, that wasn't *her*, either. Neither was having no friends. Even though her Allie J disguise was gone, Allie still had a hard time recognizing herself. She couldn't even remember who she was before all of this. What had made her laugh? What had she liked to eat? How had she decided what to wear, what kind of music to listen to? She was in the middle of a serious identity crisis. If she didn't figure out who she was soon, Shira was going to give her the one identity she didn't want: eliminated Alpha.

Allie thought she might have broken through the hate wall surrounding the Jackie O's last night, but the love fizzled as soon as Shira put the kibosh on their plan to get Sheryl Ho-bag booted out of the Academy. And so Allie was back to being lonely. She was heartbroken over Darwin and exhausted by the Alphas ostracizing her, but the person she missed the most was Charlie. Breaking up with a friend like Charlie and a guy like Darwin were painful reminders of losing her best friend, Trina, and her boyfriend, Fletcher, at the same time. It wasn't fair—why did Allie's breakups always come in twos? How was she supposed to get over a boy when she didn't have a friend to tell her she could do better?

The sound of footsteps reached her over the shrieking of the macaw—probably just Thalia, wanting to pass along some more corny words of wisdom. Allie picked up her French homework and pretended to study.

But when Allie looked up from her verb translations, the person standing in front of her wasn't Thalia but Charlie. Allie's heart leapt, then cowered. She reached for her bottle of Purell, her default security gesture. When in doubt, at least she could kill germs.

"Hi," Charlie said.

"Hi," Allie answered nervously. Was Charlie here to remind Allie (like she could possibly forget!) what a lying loser she was?

"I wanted to ask you why," Charlie said flatly. She squinted up at the sliver of moon high in the sky, barely illuminating Alpha Island, giving the place an air of mystery.

"Why what?" Allie squeaked. Was this a trap?

"Why you did it. Why you came here. . . . Why you lied."

Charlie sat down next to Allie, moving some of her books aside to make room. Allie didn't have any more to lose, so she decided to tell Charlie the truth.

She took a deep breath and started at the beginning. "I had this friend. Trina Turnbull. She and I were best friends from way back, since we were five or six years old. We played Bratz dolls together, baked cookies together. She got me through my boring childhood."

Allie paused, worrying she was already boring Charlie silly, but Charlie had a faraway, bemused expression.

"Sounds great," she said, nodding at Allie to go on.

"It was, I guess. It was fine. Anyway, my first real boyfriend, Fletcher—we were totally into each other. At least I thought we were. And Trina hung out with us all the time." Allie paused to check on Charlie again. She hadn't talked this much in days. Again, Charlie nodded at her to go on.

"She never acted jealous or anything. Maybe she was on the inside, but I didn't suspect a thing. I thought I had the perfect life. A great best friend, a cute new boyfriend . . ."

"So what happened?" Charlie asked.

"One day, the three of us went to Disneyland. Fletcher and Trina kissed. They were sitting right next to me on a ride. We went through a tunnel. It was . . ." Allie's eyes searched the rustling palm trees as she tried to find the right words.

Charlie waited patiently for Allie to continue.

"It was devastating. I lost them both at the same time. Everything I thought I had, I didn't have anymore."

"I know how it feels to be that low," murmured Charlie, her voice hoarse.

"Right. It sucks. And that's when I got the letter for Allie J. It seemed like a chance to . . ." Allie's dark blue eyes met Charlie's brown ones. "It seemed like my chance to finally be special. To escape and start over. To stand on my own two feet."

A few tears slid down Allie's cheeks and she wiped them away. She looked over at Charlie, who was staring straight ahead through the scrim of jungle plants to the flat horizon beyond. *What a relief to finally tell someone about this,* Allie thought. It felt as if the whole memory was floating away as it spilled out of her.

"I don't blame you for what you did," Charlie finally said. She turned her head and Allie was surprised to see that Charlie's eyes were glassy with tears, too. "I can relate, actually." Charlie sighed and leaned back on the chaise, staring up at the moon. "And it's amazing that you pulled it off for as long as you did."

"What do you mean, you can relate?" Allie asked. How could Charlie possibly relate?

"Oh," Charlie laughed, "you'd be surprised how much we have in common. You really want to know?"

"Um, yes?!" She pulled her sweatshirt over her knees and curled up on the chaise. She remembered something else Mrs. Wilson taught her in seventh-grade bio: that females responded chemically to sharing their lives with each other. Gabbing with girlfriends released oxytocin, which was like a happiness hormone. Maybe oxytocin was why she felt so calm confessing everything to Charlie.

"I didn't get into Alphas by receiving a letter," Charlie said ruefully. A pained smile flitted across her face like a firefly's glow, flashing once and disappearing.

"I know," Allie reminded her. "You were already here with Shira while this place was being built. It must have been amazing."

"Well, yeah, it *would* have been amazing, except Shira wasn't going to let me attend once the school was completed."

"What?" Allie was appalled. Why would AJ get in and not Charlie? Did Shira base admissions on fame alone? "But you're one of the smartest people I've ever met!"

"Shira doesn't think so. She wasn't going to let me in, even when my mom left her job to avoid the conflict of interest. She made me give up the only other person who really cared about me." Charlie's voice shook, and she looked up at Allie.

"Who?" Allie asked, not getting it. And then it hit her. "Oh." *Darwin.*

So that was why Charlie always seemed so wise and so sad. She'd given up her mother and her boyfriend, all for the chance to shine for Shira. Allie shivered in the night air as she wondered whether or not it was worth it.

"You can't tell anyone. If it ever got out, Shira would

expel me. And if that happens, all of it will have been for nothing."

"I know what *that* feels like," said Allie, looking at Charlie with new respect.

Charlie's aPod beeped, interrupting the moment before it turned into a Hallmark Channel Movie of the Week.

"Shira again." Charlie sighed. "The woman never stops!"

"Charlie?" Allie had one more question for her new/old friend. "Are you disappointed that I'm not Allie J? I mean, I know I lied to you, but were you also upset that you weren't friends with a world-famous singer?"

Charlie looked at Allie like she was one taco short of a combination plate. "Not at all. I'm glad you're *not* actually her. I liked you in *spite* of Allie J's songs, not because of them."

"So . . . you liked me . . . for *me*. Not for her." Allie looked shyly at Charlie now, suddenly embarrassed.

"Yup," Charlie assured her. "For *you*. Shira probably brought AJ here because she knew Darwin liked her music. I bet she thought AJ would guarantee that Darwin and I stayed apart. And now Shira's plan is actually working."

"Seems like it," Allie glumly agreed, remembering Darwin and AJ canoodling during lunch. But didn't Charlie want Darwin back? She was afraid to ask.

But then Charlie answered her question for her: "I'm

not going to sit back and let that happen anymore. I'll be damned if AJ is going to steal Darwin away from *both* of us."

"You don't want Darwin back for yourself?" Allie finally blurted. If Charlie was still into Darwin, she didn't want to stand in her way.

Charlie shook her head. "The truth is . . ." Charlie took a deep breath and added with a lopsided grin, "I have a new crush."

"Really? Who?" Allie squealed, thrilled to talk about someone that hadn't already broken both their hearts.

"I've been Skyping with this guy I met in Thailand. His name is Jess. He used to be this dorky kid. But now he's gorgeous. Anyway, he's sort of a computer genius, and you know I broke the surveillance system, so . . ." Charlie trailed off, suppressing a smile.

"Soooo? What are you not telling me?" Allie got up and stood in front of Charlie, sensing there was more to the story. A howler monkey hooted in the distance.

"Well," Charlie sigh-laughed, "I sort of . . . know how to fix the cameras already, but I'm pretending I don't so we can keep Skyping about it." Charlie's eyes twinkled with a look Allie recognized as happiness.

Allie was impressed. "So the broken cameras are a win-win! We get a break from Big Brother, and you get a boyfriend!" She beamed.

Charlie burst out laughing. "*Boyfriend* isn't really the right word."

"But it could be! Don't be afraid to move on. Without growth, we're just . . . wasting time." Allie put her hands on Charlie's shoulders and squeezed, looking emphatically into her eyes. "You've got everything going for you! Any guy would be nuts not to see that." Allie wrapped herself in her comforter and looked up at the stars.

"Thanks," Charlie said, smile-blushing. Her eyes twinkled. "I've been wanting to tell you about him for-*ever*."

Allie's heart did a cartwheel. They were really friends again!

"Maybe sometime I'll have a reason to go out at night again," she mused. Right now, she was so happy to have Charlie back that she hardly cared. And dwelling on the giant negative space that Darwin's absence took up wasn't going to help anyone.

"You *do* have a reason. You have to get Darwin back from AJ!" Charlie put her hand on Allie's comforter-clad shoulder. "Show him how great you are! You have a lot going on inside of you. You're like a mall that way."

Allie snorted. Finally, a pep talk that didn't make her want to gag. If there was one thing she understood, it was malls. "Are you sure it isn't weird?" she asked. "What if you change your mind about Darwin?"

"I won't. I'm sure." Charlie nodded, seeming convinced.

And Allie believed her. She didn't know how she'd do it, but it was worth a try. Maybe in time, Darwin would see past her status as imposter and discover her inner mall teeming with activity. And if nothing else, it would be a way to bond with Charlie again.

"Which reminds me, I got you something," Charlie said, reaching under the chaise longue where she'd dropped her Alpha Academy tote. She fished around in the bag and pulled out a cardboard box, shaking it like she was rolling dice. Allie squinted at it under the slivered moon, immediately recognizing Sarah Jessica Parker's face and her mass of dark blond curls.

"Ohmuhgud!" cried Allie. "It's Garnier Nutrisse number 29! Now I can get my natural color back!"

"I saw it in the theater props department and I thought it matched your roots," Charlie said. "It was this or a Demi Lovato shade of blue-black."

"Charlie, I—this is so nice." Allie's voice cracked and another couple of tears slid down her face.

"After we fix your hair, let's figure out how you're going to see Darwin again to apologize in person. Once you do that, and once AJ's real personality slips out a little more, I'm sure Darwin will reassess."

Allie could see the wheels turning in Charlie's head. She still had doubts about Darwin ever forgiving her, but Charlie was right: She might as well try. "Sounds like a plan. We renovate, then we open for business."

Charlie giggled and pulled Allie to her feet. It was time to say good-bye to her chaise longue and go back to Jackie O permanently. Having her hair back would be nice, Allie thought as she gathered up her things and followed Charlie inside. But having her friend back was even better.

18

"This is ridiculous. You two are hotter than the steam showers at the dance studio right now, and you're not even getting on the train!" Skye felt like the lead member of a three-girl pop trio as she walked slowly between Charlie and Allie, using her dance skills to balance on three-inch-heeled booties, trying not to fall on her face along the gravel path to the bubble train depot. Charlie was on her right in a bell-sleeved purple minidress with gladiator sandals, her bangs braided off to one side to show off a pair of intricate chandelier earrings. On her left, Allie's new honey-blond blow-out looked like silk in the moonlight. But tonight, Skye outshone them both. Her silver silk romper looked as if it had been poured onto her, showing off her tiny waist and ending in a strapless bandeau just under her collarbone. She had topped the ensemble off with a pair of silky red dance sleeves that looked like they came straight off a matador's outfit.

"Sorry," Charlie whispered, pausing on the walkway and cocking her head to listen for Thalia's heavy tread. It was late enough for all the campus muses to be asleep, but Skye was just as paranoid as Charlie. "Duty calls. And Allie has somewhere she has to be. Right, Al?"

"Um, yeah. Maybe. We'll see." Allie smiled brightly but still managed to look terrified.

"So, you're gonna try and grovel your way back in with Darwin?" Skye joked. She'd recently started grudgingly speaking to Allie again, after much prodding from Charlie.

"I guess," Allie said, looking hurt. "If he'll even talk to me."

Skye wanted to concentrate on the breezy caress of the warm night air across her shoulders and around her ankles, to focus on how amazing she felt in her outfit, and to think about Taz and what would hopefully be a few train cars full of people waiting for them at the depot, but Allie's voice was like a whining mosquito in her ear—demanding Skye's attention at the risk of drawing blood.

All evening, as the girls got ready for their big nights, Allie had seemed to want a gesture, a sign that Skye had finally forgiven her. Apparently an invitation to the bubble train party wasn't enough. Allie wanted more, and all night she'd been listing reasons why Skye should get over the whole Allie J fiasco and move on. After all, the mosquito whine said, Charlie had forgiven her.

"Are you ever going to stop hating me, Skye? Haven't you ever done anything crazy to get what you want?" *Buzz buzz.* Allie nearly tripped over a tree root sticking out of the ground, and she grabbed Skye's wrist, nearly taking both of them down.

"Watch out, please. My outfit is fragile. And yeah, I guess so," sighed Skye, hitching her top up higher on her torso. She didn't want a wardrobe malfunction before the party even started. "I mean, yeah, definitely."

She grimaced, thinking back to the time she snuck into the country club in Westchester, intending to take a dip in the pool with hottie surfer Dune Baxter. Throwing herself at Dune had ended in disaster. And there had been a lot of other crazy schemes before Dune. Skye thought about reckless nights sneaking into Manhattan by train, where she'd lied about her age to keep up with older kids. All the clubs she'd lied her way into just to be able to dance, or impress a boy, or get a group of girls to respect her.

"Look what I'm doing right now . . . ," she mused, smiling wanly at Allie. "I'm risking getting myself and everyone else kicked out because . . ." She paused, rolling her shoulders in their sockets and looking around at the moonlit pathway. The sounds of giggling Alphas gathered at the train depot drifted up the path and reached her ears. Suddenly, she wasn't sure exactly *why* the party train had seemed so life-or-death. What if she got kicked out? Would it really be worth it? She stared at Charlie and Allie. They blinked back at her, seemingly unconcerned. Then again, neither of them was joining her on the train. Shaking her head lightly, she brushed aside her doubts and went on. The train was on the tracks—it was too late to stop it now. "Because I want everyone to have fun. And because I want to get to know Taz." *And impress him more than AJ can*, she added silently.

She was no different from Allie, really, whose biggest crime was that she'd lied for a shot at happiness. Wasn't it possible Skye would have done the same?

Skye twirled around on one heel, looking Allie squarely in her new baby blues. "You're really pretty now that you're not in your Allie J disguise," she admitted with a smile.

"Thanks." Allie shrugged.

"No more secrets, okay?" Charlie said, obviously relieved to see Skye and Allie getting along again. "Between any of us."

"No more secrets!" Skye and Allie whisper-echoed. Skye still felt nervous about her party, but whatever the night would bring, at least Charlie and Allie would have her back. Having besties at Alpha Academy made her miss her old life so much less. The ache in her chest when she thought about her crew at BADS had almost completely disappeared. Even if everything fell apart with Taz and with dancing, at least Skye wouldn't have to face it alone. In a burst of gratitude, she pulled the two girls into a group hug, the kind she would have given the DSL Daters back in Westchester.

"To the three best Jackie O's," Skye said. "May we all get what we want tonight."

"And on that note, now that you two are friends again," Charlie said, flashing Skye an apologetic look, "I've gotta dash to Shira's. And Allie needs to go find Darwin."

"Is Shira even awake?" whispered Skye. Just saying the word *Shira* made her paranoid. Was this how the characters in Harry Potter felt when they spoke the name of You-Know-Who?

"Shira sleeps in a soundproof room with a white-noise machine that plays an exact rendition of the sounds of the Australian outback where she grew up. I've heard it—the dingoes make weird little grunts and the birds go *ooh-eee, ooh-eee*! And the crickets! Deafening." Charlie smiled and took a breath. "They're on steroids or something."

"Charlie—," Skye said, gently reminding her friend that they didn't have all night.

"Sorry, basically she needs nine hours of sleep every night, or she turns into a psycho zombie. Even more psycho than usual, I mean. She's compulsive about it."

"Mmm-kay," Skye said, rolling her Tiffany-box blue eyes. "So she's crazy. But then why do you need to go to her place *now* and miss the party?"

"Oh . . ." Charlie paused, biting her lip before admitting,

"It's ten A.M. in Thailand, which is a great time to Skype with Jess." Even in the moonlight, Skye could tell she was blushing.

"Why didn't you say so?" Skye shrieked. "Charlie and Jess, sitting in a tree, S-K-Y-P-I-N-G!"

Charlie waved at Skye and pulled Allie along the path in the direction of Shira's compound. "We'll catch up with you later—have fun!"

"I will," said Skye, just as the nearly imperceptible *whoosh* of the bubble train approaching reached her ears. Trotting down the gravel path, she rounded the corner and the jungle opened up to reveal the train depot.

Skye stared in disbelief at all the Alpha girls socializing in clumps of three or four, all waiting for *her* party to begin. Taz had really pulled this off! He'd been publicizing the big event since Wednesday, and now here he was, just around the corner, hijacking his mother's train just because Skye had asked. *How could I have ever doubted that he was the guy for me?*

Skye smiled hellos to all the loyal attendees, watching their faces fill with envy-appreciation as they checked out her outfit. As she joined a whispered conversation among Sadie, Olivia, and Matilda (a chef, a comedienne, and a shoe designer, respectively), the *whoosh* of the bubble train got louder.

Time to get this party started! Skye's spirits soared. Even if AJ bothered to show up, she couldn't ruin this for her.

Finally, the train came to a stop at the depot, its cars vibrating in anticipation. Taz stuck his head out of the first car, looking gorgeous as always in a striped Kangol cap. Skye's heart did a backflip.

"All aboard, girls!" he yelled. He smiled when his eyes met Skye's. His dimples were deep enough to swim in. Skye wanted to take the plunge and never get out.

"Thanks," she said breathlessly, taking his hand and climbing aboard.

Skye waited for the train to fill up, craning her neck out the window and watching as at least thirty of her classmates got on. She also spotted AJ rushing down the pathway toward the depot, wearing one of her usual white peasant dresses straight off the Goodwill rack. She hopped onto the last car just before the train pulled away, determinedly clambering aboard like Skye's party was as once-in-a-lifetime as attending President Obama's inauguration. For someone who made such a stink about being your own person, she sure seemed to care about being in the right place at the right time.

Watching AJ, Skye bit the inside of her cheek. *At least she's in the caboose!*

Taz cranked up the music and soon the train was rolling full speed ahead to the beat of "Party in the U.S.A.," a song that usually bugged Skye but that seemed just right to start out tonight.

The party was more awesome than Skye could have ever hoped. Girls were hopping from car to car, moving in time to the music. When the chorus landed, everyone sang along.

"If you end up in a train car with a Brazille Boy, you have to kiss him!" one of the Michelle Obamas shouted, ramping up the chaos and competition another notch.

Once all the girls seemed to get into the spirit of the game, they began lunging for the nearest Brazilles—Mel and Dingo. Mel pushed past Skye and ran for the next train car, yelling over his shoulder to Dingo, "You go back, I'll go forward! If we split up, we can cover more ground and sample more lips!"

As Miley's twangy guitar strings thrummed through the air, Skye felt a pair of muscular arms wrap around her toned shoulders.

"Hi," Taz said, his breath tickling her ear. "Rules are rules. We have to kiss."

Gladly, thought Skye, turning her head and closing her eyes as he leaned his face toward hers. *Ohmuhgud, the big lip-kiss!* Skye's limbs turned to molasses as Taz pressed his pillowy lips to hers. They slid for a second on Skye's gloss, but pretty soon they felt like they belonged there. Taz's lips tasted faintly of chocolate, and his kiss was as confident as the rest of him—not overly aggressive or rough, but not limp or fish-lipped, either. Skye's skin tingled all over, and she felt weightless, as if the train had suddenly become an antigravity chamber.

They pulled away from the kiss at the exact same time, and Taz gave her a now pink-tinted grin as the train car filled up with roving passengers. *Ohmuhgud! Hawtness!* Skye's heart did the cabbage patch as Taz squeezed her hand in his. She executed a perfect pirouette out of sheer delight. She congratulated herself for leaving Syd off the list. Things could have gotten awkward if she hadn't.

"Hey, Skye." The scratchy baby-toned voice behind her was unmistakable, even over the pounding of the train's sound system.

Skye whipped around and planted her feet in second position, her power stance.

"Hey." She hate-smiled at the diminutive diva. AJ had to have made her way through fifteen crowded train cars to get here, and it showed. Janis Chop-lin looked as if Simon Cowell had just ripped her a new one. Her tiny mouth was pursed and her forehead was creased with worry.

"Have you seen Darwin?" AJ asked hopefully, peering around Skye in hopes that there were more train cars up ahead.

"Uh-uh," said Skye, playing dumb. She wasn't going to ruin Allie's chances at forgiveness by putting AJ on the scent. "He's not here?"

"He said he'd probably make it. . . ." AJ frowned, pulling out her phone. "I texted. . . . Maybe when he writes back I should tell him that we'll pick him up?"

Before Skye could even come up with an answer of faux sincerity, AJ's phone beeped. She scooted closer to AJ and peeked over her shoulder at her phone.

Darwin: Can't come right now. Maybe later. Gotta talk to Allie and clear the air.

Ohmugud! Both AJ and Skye gasped. Allie did it! She'd convinced Darwin to hear her out.

Skye was happy for Allie, but even happier that AJ was being dissed.

"What is he talking about?" AJ whined, frantically texting back. "I'm a multiplatinum artist! This does not happen to me. I don't get stood up!"

Skye swallowed a smile. "Never woulda guessed."

"I need to get off this train," AJ coldly demanded. Her moss-green eyes darted helplessly around the car.

"We can let you off." Skye felt the stirrings of brilliance ripple through her arms and legs. It was almost too easy. And the best part was that AJ's loss would be Allie's gain. "Right, Taz?"

Taz turned around in the conductor's chair. "You're the boss!" he yelled over the music. "Time to Pretend" by MGMT blasted out of the train's loudspeakers, and he pushed a button on the steering panel that said BEACH DEPOT.

"Just . . . we can only open the doors of the caboose," Skye lied, lowering her voice so only AJ could hear her. "The others make too much noise, and we're too close to Shira's place to risk it."

"Fine. I'll be waiting there," growled AJ, turning on her heel and hurrying toward the caboose.

Counting slowly to fifteen, a delicious smile spread over Skye's face. When she was sure AJ had made it all the way through the train, her turquoise eyes focused on a long bank of red levers on the wall marked DOOR LOCK underneath. *Score!* Quickly glancing over her shoulder to make sure nobody saw her, she found the switch for the caboose and pulled down on it, locking the door to AJ's car. *Ha! See if she ruins another party now!*

"AJ just texted me." Skye giggle-danced back over to Taz. "She's staying on the train after all." It was her party. The least she could do was help out Allie in the process. And if she wounded AJ at the same time, well, that was the way the vegan cookie crumbled.

19

Charlie's eyes had gone from twinkling to bloodshot and the bags underneath them were bigger than Shira's Birkin. She looked longingly at Jess's face on the computer screen and tried to smile-swallow a yawn. It was barely noon in Thailand, judging by the bright blue sky and the blindingly white sand on the beach outside Jess's window. She didn't want Jess to think she was bored—she was far from it! During their forty-five-minute conversation, Jess had made her feel more interesting—and interested—than anyone had since, well . . . she didn't want to think about that. He was riveted by her stories about Alpha Academy, and she had been catching up on his life in Phuket.

"So Skye planned this huge party for tonight, actually, and managed to get Taz to commandeer the bubble train. There are at least thirty Alphas plus some Brazilles aboard right now. . . ." Charlie lowered her voice in a fit of paranoia.

"Wow, sounds risky."

"It *is*. I think I'm getting an ulcer. I'm not much of a risk taker." *Except for that whole dumping-my-boyfriend-to-come-here thing*, she thought.

"Hey, guess what?" Jess said brightly. Charlie suppressed another yawn and hoped it didn't look like she'd just farted. "My dad is going to the US over Christmas to look at a new manufacturing plant. I was thinking we could make a little pit stop to say hi to Shira . . . and to you." His eyes sparkled in anticipation, the way Charlie's did before it had gotten so late. "If you want, I mean."

Charlie's heart bounced like a Ping-Pong ball set free in her rib cage. "Of course, I'd love to see you!" Her ears began to burn with embarrassment when she realized she'd used the word *love*.

Ohmuhgud. She had practically just told Jess she loved him. *Delete, delete!* Charlie frantically tried to think of how to backpedal.

"I mean, that would be fun," she tried lamely, running a hand through her brown waves. Jess seemed unfazed and started looking through his iPhone to check on the dates of the flight, but Charlie was still reeling.

When she thought *love*, she thought Darwin. The first time they'd said "I love you" and meant it romantically was just last Valentine's Day. Darwin had DIYed a feast for them and had even baked a heart-shaped flourless chocolate cake.

They'd watched the sunset from the lawn in Shira's backyard, listening to the slap of the waves against the kayaks tied up on the dock. Charlie had her head in Darwin's lap, and he'd been playing with her hair, when he just came out and said it.

"I love you, Char." It had been so natural and normal that Charlie hadn't even blinked. She just said it right back to him.

"I love you, too."

It was a perfect moment. *I'll never have that easiness again with anyone*, Charlie caught herself thinking. *Nothing will ever be pure like that, not anymore.*

Lost in thought, Charlie's gaze had wandered away from the laptop and from Jess. She was staring at a black monitor on the corner of the desk, projecting the movie of her life onto the darkened screen.

"Charlie?" Jess said. "You okay?"

Snap out of it! Charlie thought-shouted. When would her heart follow her brain's instructions and just move on? She yanked her attention back to the Skype screen, gluing a smile on her face.

But just as her mocha-colored eyes focused on Jess's espresso ones, his video-box dissolved into black pixels and a new screen popped up like a rabbit from a hat.

Huh?

Charlie was smiling straight at Shira!

Charlie swallowed a babysitter-confronting-an-axe-murderer scream.

"Shouldn't you be asleep?" Charlie feigned calm, but inside she was spinning out of control.

"Shouldn't you be fixing my cameras?" Shira spat back, mocking Charlie's faux-concerned tone and mimicking her American accent.

"Uh, I almost have it, really—"

"This was a mistake. You've been wasting my time. I knew you didn't have it in you to understand this sophisticated technology. I'm going to call Steve Jobs and see when his people can come." Shira sighed and began punching commands into her smart phone, the frizzy mass of her hair flying out in all directions.

"Wait! Shira, I'm almost there—"

"How much longer can I be expected to wait?" the mogul demanded, narrowing her eyes at Charlie. "I was wrong to let you attend my school, Charlie. You are simply not Alpha material. I don't know what I was thinking, giving you this assignment. Forget about all those classmates of yours who are undoubtedly sneaking around at the moment; I should kick YOU out!" Shira stood up and leaned her whole body over the camera, planting her fisted hands on her hips.

Charlie's Ping Pong–ball heart was now in jackhammer mode. In the dim light, the mogul wasn't wearing her ubiquitous sunglasses. If Charlie made full-visibility eye contact with Shira while she was this angry, she might disintegrate on the spot.

Every cell in her body on panic overload, Charlie did the only thing she could.

"I can fix them! I know how to do it!" she cringe-yelled.

"Then do it, damnit! I need those cameras up IMMEDIATELY, Charlie Deery." Shira leaned even closer to the screen and Charlie froze as she stared at her furious ice-blue eyes. "It's those cameras or you!"

"Just give me fifteen minutes," Charlie said quietly. She needed as much time as possible, so she could warn her fellow Jackie O's to get everyone home and tucked into bed.

"You have *twelve* minutes. Effective immediately." Shira switched off her webcam. As soon as the Skype screen dissolved into black, Charlie reached for her aPod with shaking hands.

Charlie: SOS 911 SOS 911!!! Shira awake, cameras about to go back on. Get off train ASAP or we all get the X!!! You have 10 min!!! Plz confirm you got this.
Skye: Msg rcvd. Running home!

In truth, Charlie had fixed the cameras days ago, so when eleven and a half minutes had passed, she took a deep breath, clenched her teeth, and hid her eyes behind her hands as she flipped the switch that would activate full-

175

island surveillance. One by one, sixteen monitors instantly buzzed to life, each split into four quadrants showing a different view of Alpha Academy. Charlie searched the screens with her heart in her throat, desperately scanning them for evidence of life. But she couldn't find a single swishing miniskirt, swinging door, or non-sleeping Alpha girl anywhere. All the sixty-four screens revealed was darkened bedrooms full of sleeping Alphas. The rest of the island was as untouched as a bran muffin in a sea of cupcakes. Charlie finally exhaled, sitting back in the chair and grinning at just another uneventful night on Alpha Island.

"Good work, Charlie." Shira opened the basement door at the exact twelve-minute mark.

"Thanks," Charlie squeaked, still partially holding her breath.

Shira shuffled down the stairs in mink-lined mules and a beige cashmere bathrobe, an eye mask askew on her forehead holding back auburn spirals of hair. Charlie tentatively brought her eyes up to the mogul's face. She looked past the flakes of Dead Sea Algae treatment Shira habitually smeared on her frown lines and crow's-feet and searched her eyes as they scanned each and every monitor for offenders. There, in the pale blue orbs under Shira's sleep-puffed lids, Charlie thought she saw what she had been searching for since she was a little girl: a glimmer, a gleam, a gaze that all added up to the same thing—Shira Brazille was *impressed.*

"Everything looks like it's in order at the moment. I suppose you're relieved, Charlie."

"I'm happy if you're happy," Charlie murmured. The statement couldn't have been more true.

"I misjudged you on this. You had it in you after all." Shira cleared her throat and flashed Charlie the kind of smile she used for guests on her talk show—a smile full of kindness, warmth, and charisma. Most people only ever saw it on billboards or on their TVs. "Your teachers at the lab are quite impressed with your work, Charlie. It hasn't completely escaped my attention, you know."

Charlie was so surprised she could barely speak. She looked away, savoring this moment. "I'm glad," she managed.

Charlie squeezed her lips together to hold back a smile. She didn't want to get greedy. Shira's respect was a delicacy that could wither and turn sour in a millisecond. Charlie would hold this moment in her heart for the rest of her life. She wanted to be careful not to say too much and destroy it. *Shira just gave me her blessing. And to think, it only took fourteen years.*

20

It was just like *How to Lose a Guy in 10 Days*, one of Allie's favorite rom-coms. Like Kate Hudson, Allie had confessed her whole elaborate scheme. Now, like Matthew McConaughey, only way cuter and without an elaborate scheme of his own, Darwin would have to forgive her. Actually, Allie reminded herself as the jungle gave way to the narrow stretch of pebbly beach where she was supposed to meet Darwin, a lot of rom-coms ended up that way. After a bunch of misunderstandings and mishaps that tore the beautiful couple apart, all the silly little lies the characters told became water under the bridge. And the leading man fell for the leading lady that much harder because of everything they'd been through together.

Allie was ready for her rom-com resolution, hopefully followed by a kiss-and-make-up moment. She Purelled in anticipation, applied some Lip Venom plumping gloss, and tossed her back-to-blondish hair from one side to the other to make it full and beach-tousled. The wind had picked up, and out on the beach it was now blowing fast and furious. Allie wished she had thought to bring a jacket to wear over her sleeveless top.

She picked up a few stones from the beach and tossed them tentatively into the water.

Where was Darwin? Allie shuddered as a terrible thought crossed her mind: What if he had dragged her out here just to stand her up? Over the past week, she had come to understand for the first time in her life what it meant to be a social bottom-feeder. People would do all sorts of mean things to you if they thought they were justified, and she had hurt Darwin worst of all. She didn't think he was the type to pull a date-and-ditch, but it was impossible to be sure.

Allie wrapped her arms around her torso, trying to keep warm. She scanned scrubby trees that bordered the beach, willing Darwin to materialize, and went over the talking points in the mini speech she'd been giving in her head for days.

Talking Points

- Allie is like the cargo hold of a 757—full of baggage. Luckily, so is Darwin! They can unpack together.
- Forgiveness is like butter. A little goes a long way, and it makes everything taste better.

- Seeing Darwin with AJ is like watching an adorable puppy playing with a skunk. Sooner or later, things are going to stink.
- Allie is like a mall. She has a lot going on inside of her, and for a limited time, everything is on sale.

When she finally spotted Darwin walking down the path, he smiled at her, his teeth as white as the hoodie he wore over a pair of relaxed jeans.

"Hey," he said. His hair flopped sweetly in his eyes until the wind lifted it up and blew it back into place. There was no toothpick in Darwin's mouth, but Allie could smell cinnamon on his breath. It smelled like hope.

"Hey." Allie's heart raced and her fingers tingled. She could hardly believe he was giving her another chance, but since he was here with her all alone, her mind leapt to the only logical conclusion of the evening: that he still liked her, too.

"Thanks for coming. It means a lot." Allie ran her fingers through her hair, but they got stuck in a snarl. The combo of a fresh bleach job and a windy beach didn't make for smooth tresses. She pulled her hand out of her tangled hair as gracefully as possible, hoping her voice wouldn't shake much when she gave her mini speech.

"Sure. I wanted to tell you—"

"Wait," Allie interrupted. What if Darwin was going to say something bad? She needed to explain herself, and fast. "Let me say a few things first. I owe you a huge apology. The biggest apology of all time, actually. I'm sorry for lying to you. I—I know there is, like, *no excuse* for impersonating a pop singer to get into this school, and for letting you believe I was someone I wasn't . . . but except for my name and the singing and stuff, it was all me." She looked into his eyes to see if anything she said was making an impact, but Darwin was staring at the horizon like he was Free Willy getting ready to swim home.

"And"—Allie decided she might as well hit a few more talking points, so she continued, pacing along the beach— "I'm actually a really loyal person. I may not be a songwriter, or even really know yet what I'm good at, but I think I will be good at something someday. I have a lot going on inside of me."

She snuck a look at Darwin to see how he responded to this statement, but his face was as unreadable as Allie's French conjugation worksheets.

"And, um, I think that if you can find it in your heart to forgive me, which I know will be really, really tough . . ." She tried to get a read on his forgiveness quotient, but he was just standing there staring at the ocean, adorable but inscrutable. "We could start over, and really get to know the real us."

Darwin took a breath and opened his mouth, and Allie crossed her fingers on both hands behind her back. Waiting was torture! Then she crossed her toes, too.

"Oh, crap."

Huh?

But then she followed his gaze and saw a small green light glowing in a palm tree just a few feet away.

Before Allie had time to fully digest what was happening, Darwin sprang into action. He unzipped his hoodie and threw it over her head like she was 50 Cent on the way to a court appearance. That was when it finally clicked for Allie. *Ohmuhgud, the cameras are on!*

And then came his cinnamon-scented whisper in her ear: "Now we run."

Staggering along the beach wrapped in Darwin's arms and unable to see a thing through the thick fabric of his Old Spice–infused hoodie, Allie told herself not to scream. She needed to get out from under Darwin's sweatshirt, delicious as it smelled. A lifelong semi-claustrophobe after accidentally locking herself in a bathroom at the Red Lobster when she was seven, Allie didn't even like closing the dressing-room door all the way in Victoria's Secret. There was only so long she could stand being wrapped up like a mummy before passing out from panic. Already, her lungs felt like they were collapsing.

"Darwin?!" she sputtered. "I need to see! I need air!"

"Just a minute," he whisper-panted. "There are cameras all over this beach!"

As Allie tried to fight off the feeling that her world was closing in on her, it dawned on her: Charlie had sold her out! But why?! It didn't make sense. Unless . . .

Ohmuhgud, Charlie still has feelings for Darwin.

Allie may have gotten away with a giant lie, but what Charlie had done was worse. *I've been set up!* Allie struggled to control her breathing as her thoughts spun wildly under Darwin's hoodie. *And now I'm going down.*

21

CENTER FOR THE ARTS
THEATER OF DIONYSUS
SATURDAY, SEPTEMBER 25TH
2:19 P.M.

"Again, ladies! And this time stay *on* the beat! This isn't a soccer field! You're not Beckham and the rhythm isn't a ball—so why are you chasing after it?" Mimi clapped her hands twice, her bangled wrists jingling like sleigh bells. She looked at Skye and her eyebrows shot up so high they almost vanished behind her hair. Shaking her head, she obviously thought Skye was the worst of the bunch. What else was new?

Skye plastered on a fake smile and moved into first position, too tired to care about impressing Mimi today. Preparing to stumble her way through the sequence again, she glanced at the glowing digits above the hologram machine and saw class was almost over. *About time!* She still couldn't believe they had classes on *Saturdays*, and she had been dragging all day. She craved a long soak with a Lush Bath Bomb and an eight-hour date with her pillow. Even so, last night's party train ride was worth all of today's agony.

"SLEEEEVES!" Mimi screeched like someone had snapped the strap of her leo.

Skye stopped, wincing at the sound of her awful nickname and the Christina Aguilera–esque decibel level of Mimi's voice. "What!?" she spat. Her patience was thinner than Prue after a week on the cabbage soup diet.

"Once again, Sleeves, you are behind the beat. Do you understand how *offensive* that is to my dancer's eye?" Mimi paced as she yelled. "All of you! It's a disgrace!"

Everyone sucked harder than the cast of *New Moon* today. Everyone but Triple, of course, who wouldn't dream of risking a day's practice for a party. Skye glare-stared at Triple's long, toned legs and butt-kissy smile. She was busy scissoring at the barre while Mimi frothed her way into rage-ville.

A visual inventory of Skye's fellow dancers proved that the party and the mad dash after Charlie's text had wrought damage on everyone. Prue's hair looked like she'd stuck a fork in an electrical socket, and her posture had a bigger hunch than Page Six. Ophelia's flawless skin had sprouted three chin zits and her arms flapped through the routine like they belonged to a newly axed Thanksgiving turkey. Sadie was so sleep deprived that she'd managed to fall flat on her face at breakfast. She looked as if she'd wrestled a bowl of yogurt and lost. Strands of her hair were coated in still-wet

Dannon low-fat lemon, and her upper lip was puffier than a down jacket.

"Go home, everyone! Andrea, you too. Try not to breathe the same air as these sick sacks. And Sleeves . . ."

"Yes, Mimi?" Skye did her best to sound humble, stifling a yawn.

"Don't come back until you get some sleep, an attitude adjustment, and a good under-eye concealer!" Mimi flounced out of the studio, wrapping a scarf around her mouth and nose as she left.

Ugh!

The other dancers gathered up their things and crawled into track suits or yoga pants. "*Totally* worth it," yawned Prue. "I kissed Dingo! At least I think it was Dingo . . ." She looked around for confirmation, as if one of the bun-heads would know which of Shira's identical twins she'd locked lips with.

"Well, it wasn't Taz!" giggled Skye. "Because he was all mine."

"I kissed Dingo, too," Ophelia admitted, grinning at Prue as she stuck two chopsticks into her hair to hold it in place. "*And* Melbourne."

"Ah-mazing!" Skye stretched her hamstring as the sweaty group stepped into the elevator. "Tomorrow, let's start planning the next one. Today, I'm all about sleep."

The elevator doors opened and Skye twirled out into the bright afternoon, still buzzing with warm fuzzies for Taz in spite of Mimi vomiting negativity all over her. She didn't have to think about her dance teacher for the rest of the day, which meant a full eighteen hours (if you counted dreaming) to obsess over boys, parties, and post-party detox regimens.

"Razzma-Taz!" she sang, doing her version of Beyoncé's "Single Ladies (Put a Ring on It)" booty-shake just for fun.

"Sleeves!" Triple whisper-yelled. She grabbed Skye's arm as it wiggled, beckoning to have a ring put on it. "Kill it. Brazille Boy, three o'clock."

"Wha—?" *Ohmuhgud, is Taz here?* Skye's spirits soared. *He couldn't wait to see me again!* She spun around, squinting as her eyes adjusted to the blazing afternoon sun. "Where?"

Triple pointed in the direction of the jungle, where a Brazille Boy leaned against an açaí palm, looking at her expectantly. Skye blinked hard: Her expectation of Taz's chiseled jaw and confident smile was dashed by the reality of Sydney's lean frame and tousled hair. His brooding features were the opposite of his brother's open ones, and he looked especially tortured when he realized she'd spotted him. It was like ordering a burger and fries and getting a complicated salad instead—Syd might technically have been the better boy for Skye, but Taz was the only beefcake that would satisfy her craving.

"Oh, it's Syd." Skye stated the obvious in a flat voice. Realizing all the bun-heads' eyes were bouncing from her to Syd and back again, she managed to paste on her third faux-happy face of the day. "See you later, girls. Get some rest, mmmkay?" She strode away from the cluster of dancers, tuning out their whispered postulations and the sounds of their furiously texting fingers.

Skye took a deep breath as she approached Syd. He smiled and held out his hand, clutching a bouquet of plumerias and wild jasmine. *Smells strong, looks weird,* thought Skye.

Her face aching from the effort of the forced smile, she took the bouquet. "Thank you, Syd," she breathed through her mouth.

"I brought you this, too." He thrust a slim paperback into Skye's hand.

"Leaves of Grass," Skye read. "Walt Whitman. Um . . . thanks." She tucked the book under her arm, not wanting to make a big deal out of it, considering (1) she hated poetry that wasn't set to hip-hop beats, (2) Whitman went so far over her head in eighth-grade English class that she had to buy an old paper from Missy MacDowell at the high school. Missy famously overcharged for her so-called perfect papers, but this one only got a B- and Missy refused to give Skye a refund. Bad memories. And, most important, (3) she didn't want to give Syd the impression that she was into him, even for a moment, because (4) she was about to break his heart, like, *now.*

"What Whitman says about connecting to nature really

applies for me here, on this island," mumbled Syd. "I thought you might like it." His eyes reminded her of the ocean— deep and unpredictable. Skye took a breath and hoped she wouldn't see them fill up with salt water.

As an Alpha of the DSL Daters, Skye had boys falling at her feet since sixth grade, and that sometimes led to the inevitable squashed heart.

"Uh . . . Syd." She smiled, twirling once and landing in second position.

"Why didn't you invite me to your party?" Syd blurted, staring fiercely at a tree about a foot above Skye's head. "I mean, I know I told you it was a bad idea, but I was right. You should be focusing on you and your dancing—not on stupid stuff like parties. You're throwing your life away."

Had Syd just called parties stupid? Skye stared at him, her mouth hanging open in disbelief. Syd was *so* not the one, and now he'd proven it for the second time.

"Um, Syd?" She executed a double pirouette, regaining her confidence. "My parties aren't stupid. And I don't think I'm throwing my life away. Just the opposite, actually. Life is about having fun. And since you don't believe that, I really don't think the two of us have much more to say to each other."

Ka-blam! The words hit Syd like a punch in the stomach. Skye almost felt bad, but it had to be done.

"But—"

"I'm sorry, Syd." And she was. Sorry she had ever gotten involved with a judgmental wuss like him, who could dish it out but couldn't take it.

"You will be, if you aren't now," Syd squeaked. "Taz isn't going to care about you for more than a week. He has fem-ADD."

"We'll see," Skye said to his retreating back. She was like human Ritalin—she would keep Taz focused, and with minimal side effects.

Ping!

A text on Skye's aPod killed her peaceful moment dead.

What now???

SHIRA: REPORT TO MY OFFICE AFTER YOUR NEXT CLASS.

HAD No. 8: Mercy.

22

Allie plopped down onto the stone bench and stared up at the shimmering gold statue, a replica of Rodin's *Thinker* coated in 24-karat gold like a giant Oscar award. The grotto was at the end of a gravel walkway, in the center of a grove of poplars between the Pavilion and the dorms. Late-afternoon sun bounced off *The Thinker*'s melancholy eyes, and Allie squinted against it, wondering what he would be thinking if he were real. He was probably thinking about someone who broke his heart, just like she was. Only now she wasn't sure who had left her more heartbroken: Darwin when he ran off after depositing her at the door of Jackie O or Charlie for setting her up to get caught.

Now that Allie thought about it, she was suffering from three heartbreaks: over Charlie, Darwin, and herself. Now she'd never get to find out if she had real potential, if she could actually hack it as an Alpha. She had about as much chance of not getting kicked off the island as AJ had of showing up to class in a leather bomber jacket and snake-skin boots.

Her crazy schedule was wearing her out faster than Jessica Simpson went through boyfriends, and she was no closer to figuring out what she was good at. Today in Social Networking for Future Moguls, the girls were supposed to use Twitter to post Alphas-inspired nursery rhymes. After listlessly clicking around for a while, the highlight of Allie's day came when she settled on a few choice hate-tweets:

Roses are red, violets are blue, I trusted a friend, now I feel like poo.

Eenie meanie Charlie foe, catch a liar by the toe. When she frames you, it will show. Charlie dearest, now I know.

Charlie Charlie oh-so-gnarly, how does your cold heart grow? With evil plans and techno-scams And broken hearts all in a row.

In Romance Languages, Allie was informed she had flunked her quiz in three languages. In her Art of Excellence class, when asked to draw a picture of her life plan,

Allie drew a picture of herself working at Hot Dog on a Stick. Soon enough, Shira would most likely be dipping her in batter and frying her butt.

"If you lack vision in this class, you lack vision in life," her teacher Eunice Vanderlawn, life coach to the stars, had said. She'd given Allie a worried look, adding: "Failure isn't as hard to come by as you might think at your age." Allie didn't think failure was hard to come by at all. She lived it every day. She promised to try harder from now on, but when she imagined her future, all she saw was a blank page.

And in Iyengar Yoga and Meditation, Allie tried for pigeon pose and ended up closer to dead duck, pulling a muscle in her back that sent her into agonizing spasms for an hour afterward. It still hurt, which was why she'd stopped to rest next to *The Thinker* on her way to Jackie O. Staring glumly at the statue, Allie willed her back to stop throbbing so she could crawl between her sheets and close her eyes.

And to think she was feeling so hopeful just last night— less than twenty-four hours ago! Before the cameras blinked on and ruined her perfect rom-com makeup moment with Darwin, Allie actually thought she might find happiness again at Alpha Academy. But all she'd found last night was more exhaustion and a stronger-than-ever feeling of not belonging here. None of her nine classes spoke to her; she wasn't better than average in any of them. And at this school, surrounded by the most competitive, talented, driven-to-succeed girls on earth, just being average was the same as being a failure. Allie was an Alpha in Reverse: as insubstantial as AIR. She had no talent, no friends, and no future.

What am I doing here?

Allie beamed her question at *The Thinker*, willing him to provide some sort of answer, but his chin remained planted on his hand, his eyes fixed on some inscrutable point in the distance.

"If you're trying to start a staring contest, he'll beat you every time."

Charlie.

Allie stood up and faced her former friend, who smiled at her like nothing was wrong, like she hadn't betrayed her last night, framing her like they were sorority rivals in *The House Bunny*. In fact, Charlie looked weirdly happy to see Allie.

So you're my friend to my face, and you stab me in the back only when you're bored at night?

"So . . . ?" Charlie smiled, seemingly oblivious to the death-daggers shooting out of Allie's eyes. "What happened last night? How did everything go with Darwin? Did AJ get on the party train? Did Skye choose between Syd and Taz? Fill a girl in!"

Allie couldn't believe Charlie's nerve! Did she seriously think Allie wouldn't figure out the setup?

"You're a better actress than I am," she finally said, crossing her arms protectively over her Alpha uniform, shielding herself against Charlie's syrupy-sweet lies.

Charlie blinked, cocking her head at Allie as if to ask if she'd watched one too many episodes of *One Life to Live*. "What am I acting like?"

"A friend!" Allie exploded. "But you were never a friend! You were always just a spy for Shira, out for your own best interests. But the worst part of all of this is that you let me believe you were over Darwin! That is so . . . so . . . freaky!"

Allie stared at the ground, spotting a small brown lizard. She watched as it crawled up *The Thinker*'s leg and instantly changed from tan to gold. *How perfect.* Just like Charlie— changing colors to get what she wants. "And also, it's just sad," Allie added, turning back to face Charlie.

"What? I have no idea what you're talking about. I told you, I'm over Darwin." Charlie continued to blink her big brown eyes at Allie like she'd just sprouted a unicorn's horn, but her face had turned beet red.

"Ha." Allie smiled bitterly. "Then it would have been *nice*," she hissed, turning away from her frenemy and focusing her navy blue eyes on the lizard, which was now crawling along *The Thinker*'s arm, "to give me a warning before you turned the cameras on. A *friend* would have done that. An *acquaintance* would have done it. Only someone who was trying to get me *kicked out* would turn the cameras on at the exact moment I was about to make up with Darwin on the beach!"

"The beach?" Charlie groaned. "You were on the beach?"

"Where else would we have a rom-com make-up moment!?" Allie spat. "Don't tell me you didn't know exactly where Darwin would want to go."

"Ugh!" Charlie smacked her forehead loud enough to make Allie flinch. "Honestly, I didn't think about it. I guess I thought you were going to find Darwin and meet up with Skye on the train. I texted Skye, thinking she'd take care of—" Her eyes filled with tears as she trailed off, staring imploringly at Allie. "I'm sorry. I was really overwhelmed. I should have texted you, too."

Allie looked away, hurt and anger roaring in her ears. She wasn't going to let Charlie manipulate her any further. She'd been her pawn long enough.

"Puh-lease, Charlie." Allie's hands shook with righteous fury. She stood up, balling them into fists and shoving them roughly into her pockets. "Enough. Just admit you did it on purpose. Tell the truth." *The Thinker* kept on thinking in front of them, but Allie was done pondering this relationship. It was all just too convenient not to be true. Charlie hadn't forgotten; she just wanted Allie out of her way.

"Allie, think!" Charlie stood in front of Allie, her voice pinched and pleading. "Why would I deliberately—"

"I can't listen to this anymore. You're either lying to me,

or you're lying to yourself. Either way, we're done here," Allie snipped. She turned on her heel and stormed away, leaving a speechless Charlie in the grotto with her mouth hanging open in a perfectly round O.

Allie staggered down the gravel path away from Charlie and Jackie O. Her back was killing her. Every cell in her body cried out for rest, but the only real comfort she might find was in the Brazille compound. Darwin was the only person on the island who might still care about her, and she was determined to tell him what Charlie had done—even if it was her last move before getting expelled. So what if the cameras caught her now?

Allie had no business being at the Academy. The only talent she had was picking terrible friends.

23

By the time Charlie ran all the way to the beach, everything burned: her lungs, her legs, her eyes, and her heart. She wanted to cry in peace, where nosy Alpha girls wouldn't catch her in the act and start the inevitable cascade of gossipy texts that followed every piece of news at the Academy.

Her legs, rubbery from the sprint down the walkway, automatically propelled her to the spot on the beach where she and Darwin used to hang out. But for the first time, she didn't watch the gentle waves lap the pink sand and think about him. Not his lip freckle, not his goofy jokes, not even the safe feeling of his arms wrapped around her. Today, Charlie was thinking exclusively about Allie.

How could Allie jump to such awful conclusions about her? How could she accuse her of doing something so callous and manipulative? How could she toss Charlie's friendship away like expired, clumpy mascara? The fact that she hadn't even let Charlie explain herself proved just how little she'd trusted Charlie to begin with. Charlie's eyes welled up with tears as she absently traced broken-heart shapes in the sand.

Plop!

Plunk!

Whiz!

A rock flew by, just missing Charlie's ear. It skipped along the surface of the water before plunging in, rippling the glassy surface of Shira's woman-made sea. Charlie looked over her shoulder through her bangs, and her teary brown eyes made contact with Darwin's wary hazel ones. It was almost scary how Darwin always managed to turn up when she needed him. Maybe their years of togetherness had created some kind of psychic connection, even if he didn't care about her the way he used to. Charlie sobbed inwardly, feeling more hopeless and broken than ever. The invisible ties that bound them together used to be made of unbreakable steel, but now they felt thinner than dental floss.

"Hi," she managed. He sat down next to her in the sand. It was almost like they were still a couple; his movements in relation to hers were automatic, embedded in his muscle memory.

"Hey."

"What are you doing here?" Charlie didn't dare look into

his eyes again. If she did, her sprinkling of tears would turn into an avalanche.

Darwin shifted in the sand. "I'm hiding."

"From who?" Charlie stole a sidelong glance at him from under her bangs. Darwin didn't used to be the type of guy to hide from his problems.

"Allie."

Which one? Life had become so confusing. Charlie hardly knew who was who anymore, or what anyone really wanted. She longed for the days before Shira started the Academy, when she knew her place in the world and among the Brazilles. When she and Darwin were twelve and just starting to be a real couple, things had been so simple. They were gaga for each other, and the world was their playground. They played cards for hours on transatlantic flights, knowing that wherever Shira dragged the entourage, they would discover it together. It was only once their world had shrunk to the size of this little island that they had become distracted by everyone else.

"AJ or Allie A?" Had he finally realized that AJ's eco-shtick was as artificial as the beach they now sat on?

"Allie A. She wants to talk." Darwin sounded a lot like the way Charlie felt.

"And . . . you don't want to?" Charlie assumed it had gone well between Allie and Darwin last night, at least until the cameras came on.

He sighed loudly. "Last night, I met her on the beach—"

"I know," Charlie murmured. "I heard."

"But that's not the whole story. I was trying to tell her I wasn't interested. And then the cameras went on, and . . . well, she probably told you the rest. Now she thinks I'm into her, and I'm definitely, *definitely* not."

"Wait." Charlie turned to look at Darwin's profile, wondering how the boy she knew so well had become so unreadable. "You mean you don't want to get back together with Allie?"

"Uh-uh." Darwin shook his head vehemently, and a sunbleached thatch of hair fell into his eyes.

"So . . . why did you meet her and give her false hope? Why not just keep avoiding her?" Charlie felt hurt on Allie's behalf, shivering at the thought that Allie had come all the way down here expecting to really open up, only to be tossed away unopened like a piece of junk mail.

"For closure. It seemed like the right thing to do to tell her in person." Darwin looked sideways at Charlie. The next part of the sentence remained unsaid, but they both heard it. *Unlike the way you dumped me.*

"The right thing to do would be to hear her out," Charlie said gently, burying her feet in the sand as she talked. "Before you make up your mind, I mean."

Darwin snorted incredulously. "Come on, Charlie. She lied. End of story."

"Yeah, but . . ." Charlie groped for the words to explain things on her ex-friend's behalf. "She had to lie to get into this school. This was her one chance, and she took it."

"Irrelevant. She lied to all of us! If you trust her now, that's your mistake." Darwin threw a large white stone into the water and they both watched the ripples travel across the water's glassy surface.

"She would never lie to you again, I know it. And besides, unlike AJ, whose whole personality is a lie, Allie is actually a really good person. There's no comparison between the two."

Convincing your ex to date your ex-friend is definitely weird, but it's easier than watching both of them keep messing everything up.

"At least AJ is who she is," Darwin sighed, flashing an angry look at Charlie. "I'm done hanging out with girls I can't trust."

Darwin's comment stung worse than the time she'd mistaken a bottle of surfboard sealant for eye drops. She had never meant to lie to him! They had vowed always to be honest with each other, but that was before Shira had forced her to trade her boyfriend jeans in for a shiny pleated skirt, and her boyfriend in for a spot at the Academy.

"You're making a mistake. Allie is a great girl. Even though she's mad at me right now, I still consider her a friend."

"Why is she mad at you?" he asked suspiciously. "What did you do?"

I'm a good person, she wanted to shout. *I didn't do anything!*

"She thinks I turned on the cameras last night on purpose to get her in trouble. I guess she thinks I'm still into you . . . because of why we broke up."

The silence between them was suddenly thicker than Triple's foot callouses. Charlie could feel Darwin's eyes on her as she stared hopelessly out at the ocean, willing him not to ask the next logical question.

"Wait. Why *did* we break up?"

Uh-oh. Charlie had always told herself that if Darwin ever asked her directly what had happened, she would have to tell him the truth. It was what she would have wanted from him if the situation were reversed. And, she reasoned, maybe it would help him move on, or at least help him hate her less. Or . . .

She barely allowed the thought to flit across her conscious mind before shoving it back down into the portion of her brain where pointless wishes belonged: Maybe it would mean they could be together again someday.

"You really want to know?" Charlie's voice wavered, pinched with emotion.

"I deserve the truth," Darwin said flatly, shifting in the sand so he was sitting between her and the ocean. "Don't you think?"

Okay, thought Charlie. *Fine.* But how was she supposed

203

to put it? *I broke up with you to become an Alpha. So I could go to high school near you and not be shipped off to a boarding school. So I could make something of myself. So I could finally show your mom that I deserve you.*

"Your mom made me," she cough-confessed, looking up at the robin's egg–blue sky. It was as simple as that, sadly. Shira held all the cards. Always had. Probably always would.

Charlie lowered her eyes back to Darwin and waited for a look of relief to wash over Darwin's smooth, tanned face. She sat up straight, all thoughts of Allie vanishing like a scarf up a magician's sleeve. She held her breath, expecting Darwin to reach out, to grab her and hold her tight, his voice in her hair saying how much he appreciated the sacrifice she had made for him. She waited for awe, amazement, and maybe even renewed devotion. Maybe now he would be willing to wait with her for her year at Alpha to be over, for Charlie to prove to Shira that she was worth his time.

But Darwin didn't say any of that. Charlie watched as his face hardened, closing up like an oyster. Instead of bringing them closer together, the truth was making things between them even worse.

"I. Can. Not. Believe. You." Darwin's nostrils flared as he slowly spit out the monosyllables. His ears blazed neon pink. "She controls *everything*! Why did you have to let her control this, too?"

"But I did it for us—" Charlie's spine sagged and she

curled into herself, defeated, tears streaming down her face. "You don't know what it's like not to have the world in the palm of your hand, Dar—"

"Don't tell me what I know," he spat, hurling his body up from the sand until he stood towering above her. "In fact, don't tell me anything. I went over and over this in my mind, trying to figure out what I'd done wrong, what could have possibly pushed you away. And all the time—it was her?" His eyes wet with tears of his own, he backed away from her like she was a grizzly bear about to attack—scary, potentially insane, and capable of ripping him to shreds.

"Wait!" she cried, jumping to her feet and staggering after him. "You don't understand!" But he waved her off and began to run back up the beach toward his house and the security of Shira's constant surveillance, where Charlie wouldn't dare go.

She watched him run through a screen of her tears, waves of shock rippling through her from the boulder he had thrown into her emotional ocean. She'd finally gotten everything she thought she wanted—a place at Alpha, respect from Shira, and for Darwin to know the truth.

So how come she felt like she had nothing at all?

24

Skye fidgeted in an uncomfortable straight-backed chair outside Shira's office, staring at an enormous metal sign that read BRAZILLE INDUSTRIES: EMPOWERING WOMEN EVERYWHERE in thick laser-cut letters. She crossed her legs and then uncrossed them, leaning her weight on one butt cheek and then the other in a desperate attempt to relax. She wondered how many minutes she had waited so far—five? Ten? Ten thousand? Time had lost all meaning in this elegant little room just a few feet from the epicenter of all things Shira.

A laptop sat open on the unmanned reception desk, its Apple symbol pulsating like a sinister heartbeat. It reminded Skye of an Edgar Allan Poe story she'd read in her seventh-grade English class. She was now living her own non-murderer's version of "The Tell-Tale Heart," and it was only a matter of time before her own paranoia caused

206

her to accidentally confess, to mess up and say something she would later regret. Even if Shira hadn't summoned her here to expell her, Skye would probably blurt out one of the many infractions she'd committed lately. Skye fretted and picked at her cuticles, doing her best to forget all of her Alpha Academy crimes before Shira got her to spill. She decided the safest approach to an interrogation session would be to list all the potential infractions Shira might accuse her of and counter each one with an excuse Shira would buy.

ACCUSATION: Skye threw a party on the bubble train!
EXCUSE: Skye was awakened in the Jackie O bedroom by a noise outside. Some girls stole the train and she jumped on to make sure no one got hurt. She comes from a long line of Metro-North train conductors and thought she could help.

ACCUSATION: Skye was a disaster in dance class today!
EXCUSE: Skye had a high fever and stomach cramps. Possibly swine flu. She dragged herself out of bed and forced herself to dance through it because that's what a true professional would do. Shira should put her in quarantine, not make her leave school! Swine flu at Alpha Academy would be a public relations nightmare,

and Skye would hate it if someone leaked it to the
press, hint hint!

ACCUSATION: Taz commandeered the *Joan of Ark* for
Skye!
EXCUSE: Joan of *who*? There's a *lake* here?

ACCUSATION: Skye had used her keys to the dance
studio to throw a party there!
EXCUSE: Shock and dismay! Skye would *never* violate
a sacred dance space like that! Skye had gone to
the studio at night, but only because she needed to
practice her routines. She was an Alpha and therefore
she was determined to be the best. Wasn't that why
Mimi had given them the key? So they could practice
at all hours?

Just when Skye thought she couldn't take another second,
Shira's office door slid open. Skye leapt to her feet, clearing
her throat and stretching her lips into what she hoped looked
like the smile of an honest person with nothing to hide.

But her smile faded as quickly as it appeared, because
instead of Shira or one of her many assistants, several of her
classmates began to shuffle out of the office, each one rolling a suitcase. Skye could practically smell the shame and
disappointment wafting out of their pores.

"We're all going home," Jojo, a ukulele prodigy, told her. Her slate-gray eyes were filled with tears, and her face looked puffy, like she'd been crying for a long time. "Nice meeting you," Jojo whispered. "Look me up on MySpace if you get kicked out, too—I'm starting a former Alphas support network."

Ohmuhgud! Skye grabbed her hand for a secret supportive squeeze. Two Michelle Obamas, an Oprah, a Meg Whitman, and two Hillary Clintons followed Jojo into the foyer.

"This is really all her fault," hissed one of the Hillaries Skye couldn't recall the name of (actually, wasn't her name *Hillary?*). She pointed a French-manicured finger at Skye. "It was her stupid party."

"Skye Hamilton! Enter!"

Skye's heart began an intricate Savion Glover tap routine inside her ribs.

Gulp! Skye pushed her way past the last of the expelled Alphas. Walking into the room, she noticed right away how silent it was. *Tomblike,* Skye thought, vowing to push any more Poe references to the back of her mind for now. The carpet was thicker here in Shira's office, the walls lined in a more expensive, shinier kind of wood. Skye took a deep breath and smelled Shira's perfume; she was wearing Money, the first of several perfume lines launched by X-Chromosome. Skye remembered the ad campaign, which featured Leighton Meester and Ed Westwick rolling around in piles of cold hard cash.

Skye waded through the ultra-plush carpet and approached Shira's enormous Australia-shaped desk. Light streamed in from the windows behind the mogul, causing her to look like a silhouette.

"G'day, Skye." Shira's voice wasn't quaking with anger. She sounded strangely friendly, actually. But Shira loved to catch people in verbal traps on her talk show, and Skye wasn't naive enough to take her friendliness at face value.

Deny, deny, deny! Skye pinched the inside of her wrist with the fingers of her other hand so as not to blurt out a hasty apology before Shira even accused her.

"Sit, please," Shira said. Skye sat. Skye's heart abandoned its tap routine and went into hyperdrive, like it was trying to win an episode of *So You Think You Can Dance*. She wondered if it was possible to have a heart attack at age fourteen. She pictured her mother's face crumpling into sobs when she got the news of Skye's death. Her parents might have to close down Body Alive Dance Studio out of grief. Without the added income, they would have to move out of Westchester and into some horrible place like Yonkers or Riverdale. Maybe someplace even worse!

While Skye's thoughts spiraled into the South Bronx, Shira leaned forward in her chair and tapped a bloodred fingernail into the air in front of her. Skye's jaw dropped as a gold book the size of a sheet of paper suddenly materialized on an invisible screen. The holo-book floated above Shira's desk, shimmering like a magic coin. "Open. Saturday," Shira said, sounding bored and tired.

The holo-book turned into a see-through list of appointments, and Skye tried to read the backward writing.

"Conference with Michelle postponed to seven fifteen," Shira said, raising her auburn eyebrows at Skye. *Michelle Obama?*

The backward writing dissolved for a moment, then instantaneously appeared with the new appointment highlighted in green toward the bottom. Satisfied, Shira flicked the page with her index finger and sent it flying off the invisible screen.

Finally, Shira's dark lenses faced Skye.

"I brought you here, Skye, because I saw something interesting on the cameras earlier today."

Today? Skye retraced her steps from the day and couldn't think of anything she'd done that was the least bit interesting or unusual, except for telling Syd she wasn't into him. . . . Had the cameras heard her?

"I saw Sydney give you some flowers. And a book . . ."

"It's not what it looks like! We aren't—"

"Calm down," Shira said shortly. "I was *pleased* with what I saw."

Huh? Skye was lost. "Oh."

"Sydney is a very sensitive boy. And lately, I've noticed

211

a change in him. He's been happy. Happier than I've seen him in years. I couldn't figure out why until I saw his face today on the surveillance system. *You* have been making him happy, Skye. And I'm all for the two of you dating. Or, hanging out? Isn't that what you kids call it?"

"But . . . ," Skye sputtered. She winced as she heard Syd's condescending tone, when he'd called her parties stupid, echo in her ears. A shudder passed through her body as she imagined enduring his holier-than-thou speeches about nurturing her passion. The last thing she wanted was to be ordered to hang out with Syd!

"Forget about the rules. My son has never been this happy, and I'd like it to stay that way. Mirror!" An opaque square popped up where Shira's appointment book had appeared before, and Shira opened a desk drawer and pulled out a tube of X-Chromosome Queen of Hearts lipstick. She stared at the square briefly as she expertly whisked the color around her mouth, then flicked the mirror square away and pursed her newly matte red lips at Skye. "Just don't break his heart!"

But I already broke his heart! Skye had no idea what to do. You couldn't order a girl to like someone she hated . . . *could you?*

"One more thing," Shira added as she blotted on a piece of SHIRA BRAZILLE, AMERICA'S ALPHA stationery. "About your weak performance in dance class lately."

Skye's body involuntarily tightened up again before she remembered that if she had just been ordered to date Syd, she wasn't going anywhere.

"Stop giving up every time you have a setback," Shira continued. "Alphas are resilient. We keep fighting! Stay with it, stay focused, stay confident! That's how I've become the woman I am today. Don't sabotage yourself. Remember, I have faith in you." The mogul stood up and walked around her huge desk, pausing to put a hand on Skye's shoulder. It felt like Icy Hot, cool and jarring at first, but then creepily, invasively warm. Skye willed herself not to look up—seeing Shira this close to her would freeze more than just her shoulder.

The door to Shira's office opened and Fiona stuck her head inside. "Shira, your ride is here."

"I'll be watching you," Shira said over her shoulder as she followed Fiona out. "Do great things!"

Ugh! Feeling dizzy and disoriented by Shira's one-two punch, Skye watched the mogul's back as she strode away in a pair of stiletto boots. When she was gone, Skye stared at her strong, slim hands, wondering how everything she had in Westchester—the freedom to dance *her* way, the freedom to crush on whatever boy she liked, the freedom to watch TV, the freedom to be in the same room as her parents, even—had slipped out of them. Blinking back tears, Skye stood up and walked around the Australia-shaped desk to look miserably out the window at Shira's ocean view. She pressed her nose to the glass the way she always did as a kid at the dance studio, when her biggest fear was that nothing exciting would ever happen to her, that all her days would unfold predictably, ad infinitum. How she longed for some of that predictability now! As the glass fogged up with her exhalations, she imagined her graceful, elegant mother was standing on the other side of the window, watching over her.

"Help me, Mommy," she breathed, wiping a tear from the tip of her nose before it landed on Shira's pristine blood-red carpet. "What do I do now? How can I do great things when every choice I make is the wrong one?"

How could being under the thumb of the most controlling woman on earth possibly turn her into a Leader of Tomorrow or make her an Empowered Female? Skye wiped the condensation off Shira's window, revealing not Natasha Flailenkoff but a wide expanse of blue-green lawn, and in the distance, a fake, indifferent ocean.

All constructed like a chess board by a woman who thought every move was hers to decide, for whom everyone was a mere pawn to her queen. Skye shivered as a hopeless laugh escaped her lips. She knew enough to see when she had been beaten.

Checkmate.

25

Flat on her back in bed again and surrounded by her closest frenemies, Allie waited for Thalia to cue up tonight's PowerPoint of inspirational images.

"Prepare to be inspired," Thalia murmured as she manipulated some files on the touchscreen in the wall at the back of the room. She wondered what Thalia thought about her and the other Jackie O's—was she jealous of the girls who might someday be titans of industry, inspirational leaders, famous in the arts or sciences? Or did she pity them for being under the pressure, for being so willing to stab one another in the back? As if Thalia could read her mind, her golden eyes came to rest on Allie's blue ones. She smiled and put a long finger to her lips, even though Allie was pretty sure she hadn't been talking. It was like Thalia knew how loud Allie's thoughts were inside her head. Her mind had been racing all evening like an out-of-control bubble

215

train. Ever since the showdown with Charlie at the *Thinker*'s grotto, she had officially jumped the track.

Allie made an effort to take a deep, cleansing breath like they did in yoga class. *Clear your mind of clutter*, she told herself in the voice of Samsara, the gorgeous yogini who taught Alpha yoga and who recently demonstrated her ability to crack walnuts with her glutes. *Stop drinking the hater-ade!*

Settling back into her pillows and sighing loud enough for Charlie to hear, Allie stared at tonight's slideshow, hoping she would find some inspiration in it but doubting the possibility. Charlie, Triple, Skye, and AJ all lay in their beds preparing to watch, but everyone seemed distracted and only half present. Or was Allie just projecting, like Thalia was about to?

The PowerPoint began with the words *FAITH IN YOUR FUTURE*, written in the slanted Edwardian Script font Shira favored because it was both feminine and strong, just like the Alphas themselves. The phrase somersaulted across the darkened wall of the Jackie O house, followed by a series of photos with other phrases popping up on top of them. First came war orphans in Darfur, smiling and holding hands in a depressing-looking refugee camp (*THE MOST POWERFUL HOPE IS OFTEN BORN OF TRAGEDY*, read the message at the bottom), then Brazillian dancers at a carnival parade (*STRIVE TO CREATE JOY WHEREVER POSSIBLE*), then Rosa Parks and Martin Luther King, Jr. (*NEVER THINK ONE*

PERSON CANNOT MAKE A DIFFERENCE!), Sasha and Malia Obama in the White House vegetable garden with Bo (*YOU ARE THE NEXT GENERATION OF LEADERS!*), and—wait, was that Mercedes, the model with lupus from *America's Next Top Model, Cycle 2*? (*DON'T LET ROAD-BLOCKS STAND IN THE WAY OF YOUR SUCCESS!*). And, *ohmuhgud*, a picture of Jamie Lynn Spears holding her baby in their "inspirational" slideshow! (*BUT TRY TO BE A KID FOR AS LONG AS YOU CAN!*) Allie smiled, assuming this was Thalia's un-Shira-approved way of spicing up the guided meditations. Knowing these slideshows were preachy, Thalia had found a few surefire shots to keep the Jackie O's from rolling their eyes and filing their nails through the whole exercise (or in Triple's case, from using the opportunity to catch some early z's).

After the pictures faded out, Charlie's mom's British-accented voice played over an Enya song, imploring the girls to "Visualize positive outcomes. See it! Feel it! Live it! All will be manifested and your wishes will be granted. Faith in the future will take you where you need to go."

Allie involuntarily emitted a loud, incredulous snort. Faith in her future—*ha!* "Allie, Václav Havel said that the most profound doubt is what gives birth to new certainties, and that hopelessness is the soil that nourishes human hope." Thalia smiled serenely.

If that were true, Allie was fertilizing enough hope for an

217

army. As the last strains of Enya faded out and the screen went dark, Thalia added a final aphorism for the whole room. "Take the first step in faith. You don't have to see the whole staircase, just take the first step. Martin Luther King, Jr." Then she quietly padded out of the room.

"Faith in our futures? I thought our futures were now." AJ yawned.

"I used to have faith. Faith in my *friend*. A lot of good that did me." Allie glared at Charlie.

Charlie popped up onto her elbows and glared back. She looked like she had been crying; her eyes looked puffier than Jordin Sparks in a stretch leather dress. "I had faith that telling my *friend* I didn't know she was on the beach would *mean* something to her. A lot of good that did *me*."

Skye interjected, not one to be out-whined. "I had faith that Syd would be able to live without me. A lot of good that did *me*!"

Triple reached up and yanked off her eye mask so everyone could see the big brown windows to her soul roll up in their sockets. "I had faith that I'd get roommates who weren't so obsessed with their stupid problems that they couldn't even focus on why we're here!" She looked around at each one of the Jackie O's like they were something stuck to the bottom of her shoe.

"Okay, *Shira*." Skye's eyes narrowed into catlike slits.

"Yeah," piped up AJ, surprising everyone. AJ didn't

usually find much to agree with Skye about. "Give it a rest, *Andrea*."

Using Triple's real name was always guaranteed to make her pout. She pulled her eye mask back down and turned away from the group. Allie caught herself smiling at AJ and had to admit it was nice of her to stand up for everyone and make Triple stop judging everyone for once.

AJ's aPod beeped, and she opened it up to read a text. She slumped over as she read, and when she looked up, her expression was as flat as her voice. "Well, I had faith that Darwin liked me." She tossed her aPod onto the floor, sending it skittering under her bed. She picked up her guitar and started strumming a blues riff, her black hair falling over her face and hiding what Allie was surprised to see looked like real confusion and actual sadness.

Allie's aPod beeped from its charger on her gum-strewn nightstand. She grabbed it and quickly changed its setting to vibrate when she saw the text was from Charlie, who lay only three feet away.

Charlie: I bumped into Darwin on the beach. Told him how great the real Allie was. The text to AJ must mean he likes you!!! You did it!!!

Allie's face flushed immediately. Could Charlie be trusted?

Allie: Why should I believe u?
Charlie: I can't make u trust me. But I'm telling the
truth! Always have, always will.

Charlie sat up in bed and stared at Allie with a huge,
goofy grin that made her look like a Powerpuff Girl. It was
the kind of smile you could only muster if you were truly
happy for someone, the kind of grin you only gave a true
friend. Allie mirrored a tentative smile back. If what she
said was true and Allie dropped her guard once and for all,
she might get her best friend back and rekindle things with
Darwin all on the same day.

Allie: Sorry I had the wrong idea about the cameras.
It's been hard for me 2 trust. 4give & 4get?
Charlie: Deal.
Allie: Deal.

Allie's heart fluttered a little at the thought of everything
working out neatly, just like at the end of a rom-com. What
was it she had told Charlie earlier that week? If it wasn't
okay, it wasn't the end? Soon, she'd find something she was
good at, a talent that would prove she belonged at Alpha
Academy for more than just sharing a name with Allie J.
And once that happened, her mall would be officially open
for business.

26

Charlie stood at her workstation and smoothed out the wrinkles in her platinum coveralls, smiling at the cluster of nine other inventor-tracked Alphas and their mentor, Dr. Irina Gorbachevsky. She looked at the curved recycled-glass wall of the lab before continuing with her presentation, rereading the slogan etched there as if for the first time:

> *Dream lofty dreams, and as you dream, so shall you become.*

She clicked one of her makeshift teleportation pods closed. The pods were made from two metal garbage cans Charlie had stolen from the Pavilion, but even though they might look like junk, they worked perfectly. Grinning with the excitement of scientific discovery, she typed in a command on her aPod, which she'd rigged to serve as the pod's remote control. "Okay, so everyone saw me put my bracelet in, right?"

The other girls each nodded solemnly, and Charlie pushed ENTER on the keypad. The pods of Charlie's machine began to rattle and then hummed simultaneously like a dial tone on a landline.

Nine coverall-clad inventor Alphas whispered excitedly as their eyes followed Charlie across her workstation to the second pod.

"Mega awesome," murmured Yvette, a cyber-punk with spiky blue-black hair and an eyebrow piercing who had been working for months on developing a pheromone-heightening perfume that would attract only psychologi-cally compatible boys. "Charlie's on a roll."

"And now . . ." Charlie raced over to the second pod, her heart revving with excitement over her new project. With any luck, she might be just a few years away from inventing a working teleportation device. And if that happened, she would be set for life. Shira or no Shira.

She unlatched the second pod and smiled down at her cameo bracelet glinting up at her. It was the one with the empty spot where Darwin's picture used to go. She may not have a soul mate anymore, but she might just have a future. She picked it up and passed it around to the group.

"As you can see, the bracelet made the trip perfectly

intact. I'm feeling good about inanimate objects now, and I decided to try a plant a few days ago. So far the plant is doing well. I need to do some molecular testing to be sure. . . ." She stroked the leaves of the ficus she'd transported in the teleportation pod, looking around at the nodding heads of her fellow inventors. One of her mechanical butterflies sat on a leaf, its recycled aluminum wings fluttering as if it were giving her a round of applause.

"Wonderful work as always, Charlie. Highly exciting." The bespectacled Dr. Gorbachevsky nodded. Dr. G had two PhD's and was a pioneer in nanotechnology and string theory, and Charlie adored her. Dr. G blinked her raisin-colored eyes and grinned at her star pupil. "Let us know when you get the DNA testing done and then we'll talk about trying a larger life-form. A fish, perhaps."

"Nice," effused Lydia, a food scientist with a passion for cloning cuts of meat. "Let me know if you want to try throwing a steak in there—I can safety-test it after."

"Great." Charlie grinned. The lab was like a cathedral, built to inspire and awe future inventors who already worshipped technology, and she was a willing convert.

"Let's move on to Yvette's pheromones," directed Dr. G. "Keep working, Charlie." As the girls followed Dr. G to the next workstation, Charlie's laptop blinked with a chat request from Bee.

Bee: Time to chat, love? Missing you—how are things? Fill your mum in!

Charlie sat down on a stool and her fingers hovered above her keypad. Where to start? She hadn't chatted with Bee all week, and so much had happened! She looked down at her mood-influenced nail polish, which she'd licked just before her presentation. Her nails were a calm iridescent blue, perfectly reflecting her calm, peaceful state of mind.

Charlie: Hi, Mom! Things are good here. We lost a few more girls. . . .

Charlie tallied up the numbers in her head. So far, twenty-two girls had already been kicked off the island. Twenty-one once you factored in that Ivy Lambert was a fake. And more would probably be going soon. Shira wanted to find the one girl with enough potential and smarts to be as successful as she was, but there wasn't room for too many like Shira in the world. Charlie wondered if two would be chosen, or even three. She lapsed into a fantasy where Allie, Skye, and herself were the three left standing on the island by the end of the school year and were given Shira's blessing to create a new multimedia empire they would run together.

Don't get ahead of yourself. One day at a time.

Bee: But you're still there. And I got a progress report that said you earned a ride in a PAP and contributed to fixing a technology glitch!

Charlie grinned, remembering the look on Shira's face after she'd fixed the cameras. Bee didn't need to know that she'd also been the one to break them. Not now, when the lab felt more like a home than any of the hotel rooms and temporary apartments she'd lived in with Bee, and her workspace was full of things she'd created all on her own—not a bit of it belonged to Shira. And now that Allie had forgiven her, the future was all theirs.

Charlie: Yep. I got some help from a friend in Thailand.

Charlie could picture it like it had already happened: Jess and Charlie, the cute new couple, would hang out on the pink-sand beach with Darwin and Allie, and everyone would be best friends. There would be romance, friendship, and the promise of unbridled Shira-sanctioned success in her life now: It was a new time, and anything was possible. She really could have it all.

Ping!

Charlie turned away from her laptop and grabbed her aPod, switching it from teleportation mode to Alpha mode. Who would be texting her during class? Maybe it was another forgive-n-forget text from Allie? Or maybe it was Darwin, apologizing for running away from her on the beach and admitting that Allie was the best choice for him.

When the text appeared on the screen, she suddenly felt like she'd teleported a grenade directly to her stomach.

Darwin: I understand why you did it. I'm tired of my mom controlling my life. I am going to fight 4 you. 4 us. 4 ever.

Reading the text again and again in case she'd somehow misinterpreted it, Charlie's perma-grin dissolved on her lips like Alka-Seltzer in water, replaced by a nauseous, nervous certainty of her inability to stop the impending disaster. All the fantasies she'd been nurturing only a moment ago had been instantly erased by what she had just read.

Her hands shaking, Charlie typed a quick note to Bee. She needed to think.

Charlie: Sorry, Mom, gotta run. Will get back to you soon! Love u.

Staring at her blue nails, Charlie felt like a computer whose hard drive had been erased entirely. Her life would have to be rebuilt from a bunch of spare parts.

And yet . . .

Her head swam with visions of Darwin—his arms around her again, taking away all of her worries. All of their inside jokes, created over a lifetime together. The feeling that she was her best self with him, that no matter what her days held, her nights would be filled with adventures she could share with her best friend and better half.

Of course, there would be issues to work out with Allie. And Charlie couldn't imagine Shira ever approving of the two of them. And what about Jess? Was she just going to toss him aside like a cheap umbrella now that she'd found shelter from the storm with Darwin? Her head spun with the uncertainty of it all.

But the one thing Charlie was sure of was Darwin. He was the flame to her moth, the chocolate to her peanut butter, the moon to her inner werewolf. If he wanted her back, she wouldn't hesitate. She *couldn't*. And so her thumbs did the only thing her mind would let them. They typed a message back.

Charlie: Can't wait to tell u in person how happy you just made me.

Ping!

The thought of being with Darwin again was like swimming to the surface of a pool. Without him, she was just treading water, holding her breath, and trying to survive.

Now that they were back together, she could breathe again. They would find a way to make it work, Charlie thought. They belonged together, and the universe would adjust. Feeling confident in her decision and waiting for Darwin to text again, Charlie ran her finger over the cameo on her bracelet. Soon, Darwin's picture would be back inside the empty oval where it belonged, keeping her safe.

Ping!

Allie: Thanks again. So happy we made up! You're a real friend.

Uh-oh. Charlie blinked, not knowing what to say or to whom. She bit her index fingernail anxiously, then remembered to check her polish. It had turned from peaceful pale blue to bad-luck black. Her stomach clenched as she tried to imagine telling Allie that after all they'd been through, Darwin had chosen *her*. Charlie looked desperately around the lab, but there were no answers to be found here. In the space of five minutes, her life had become a giant snowball rolling down a mountain, gathering snow until it was so big it would crush everything she had built with Shira, with Jess, but most of all, with Allie.

Breaking a friend's heart or breaking her own: Those were Charlie's only two options now.

Either way, she lost.

Thousands applied.
One hundred got in.
Only one will win.

BELLE OF THE BRAWL

Who will it be? Don't miss the third novel in
the ALPHAS series—Coming October 2010.

The only thing harder than getting in is saying goodbye.

B0B262

Welcome to Poppy.

A poppy is a beautiful blooming red flower
(like the one on the spine of this book). It is also
the name of the home of your favorite books.

Poppy takes the real world and makes it
a little funnier, a little more fabulous.

Poppy novels are wild, witty, and inspiring.
They were written just for you.

So sit back, get comfy, and pick a Poppy.

poppy

www.pickapoppy.com

gossip girl   THE CLIQUE   *the* daughters

ALPHAS   the it girl   POSEUR

THE A-LIST   secrets of my
HOLLYWOOD ROYALTY   HOLLYWOOD LIFE